Hell Trail

Stranded in the desert with a lame horse, Frank Clooney hitches a ride using the alias Sam Rafter to hide his true identity as a bounty hunter. But his chance meeting with the Carver family lands him in a pile of trouble.

To say the Carvers are dysfunctional would be putting it mildly. Ned Carver is a scoundrel and a tyrant, and it soon becomes apparent that his wife sees Clooney as the instrument of her own and her daughter's freedom.

Then, Clooney finds himself on very dangerous ground when a notorious outlaw, Spitter Larch, joins them. If the sidewinder remembers who Sam Rafter really is, Clooney's life won't be worth a plugged nickel!

Glasgow Life and its service brands, including Glasgow Libraries, (found at www.glasgowlife.org.uk) are operating names for Culture and Sport Glasgow.

Glasgow
CITY COUNCIL

Hell Trail

RIO BLANE

A Black Horse Western

ROBERT HALE · LONDON

© James O'Brien 2005
First published in Great Britain 2005

ISBN 0 7090 7775 0

Robert Hale Limited
Clerkenwell House
Clerkenwell Green
London EC1R 0HT

Typeset by
Derek Doyle & Associates, Shaw Heath.
Printed and bound in Great Britain by
Antony Rowe Limited, Wiltshire

PROLOGUE

The bullet that snatched Frank Clooney's hat from his head and spun it in the air would have, had it been a couple of inches lower, taken the top of his head clean off. He had instinctively thrown himself from the saddle on hearing the crack of a rifle. His quick reflex action had saved him from an early appointment in the hereafter, with whom he was not sure. He had done enough in his time for the Devil to have an interest in his passing. He had also done enough for God to give him the once over. And at this point, with the scales for and against fairly evenly balanced, had George Watkins's bullet found its target, Clooney reckoned that there would have been a right old tussle for his immortal soul.

A second bullet followed the first, spitting grit in his face as he lay winded on the dry dusty street, hoping that when he tried to get up his bones would not crumble after the heavy fall. He shooed his horse round the side of the shack he lay outside. The bushwhacker had not yet got the idea of shooting the mare, but unless he had a hole in his head the size of an apple, the thought could not be far off coming to him.

A man without a horse in desert country was a dead man.

A third round nipped at the heel of Frank Clooney's right boot. Of one thing he was certain, he needed to make it to the cover of the nearby shack, pronto. Two more bullets chased his tail to the shack, the second one ripping a chunk from the sagging shack door that was too much for the rotten wood to absorb. The door shuddered and disintegrated in a cloud of worm-infested dust. As he dived into the shack, Clooney had spotted a curling wisp of smoke from the batwings of a saloon that now had only ghosts as patrons. The town of Good Intentions had not amounted to much in its heyday, if it ever had a heyday. Now abandoned, its crumbling buildings along the main street leaned against each other for support. One day soon the buildings at the end of the rows would grow weary of holding every other building up and fold. Then, in one fell swoop, Good Intentions would simply vanish.

'Watkins? George Watkins?' Clooney shouted.

'It's me, Clooney,' a voice confirmed from the

saloon. 'You no-good bastard of a bounty hunter!'

'Which way do you want to leave Good Intentions?' called Clooney. 'In the saddle or across it? That's all that has to be settled, Watkins.'

'I ain't going back to Tandyville to be strung up, and that's for sure. So I guess there'll only be one of us riding out of this shithole.'

'Have it your way, Watkins,' Frank Clooney called back. 'Now all that's left to decide is, who's going and who's staying put.'

'That's already decided, I reckon,' came back Watkins's reply. 'I've got a 'chester. Your rifle is still in its saddle scabbard. All you've got is a sixgun. You haven't a hope of getting near enough to me to get a telling shot off, Clooney.' He laughed harshly. 'I figure that in no time from now, I'll be pissing on your grave.'

Frank Clooney knew only too well the truth of what Watkins said. He could pop all day long with his pistol, but he might as well be trying to drown Watkins in spit.

'Well, what are you waiting for, Clooney?' George Watkins taunted. 'For me to die of old age?'

What he was waiting for was half a good idea as to how he might dislodge the man who, dead or alive, was worth $1,500. Then he saw what might be just the break he needed. In the alley at the side of the saloon, there was a drum painted black. He had seen such a drum a couple of times before and, if this drum was the same, it was a kerosene or coal-oil container. Saloons needed lots of light, and the shrewd owner often bought in bulk to keep the cost down and avoid the risk of running low on oil. Saloons were normally full of temptation, but a poorly lit saloon was right for all sorts of evil-minded *hombres* getting all sorts of evil ideas, like slitting the 'keeper's throat and snatching the takings.

Clooney knew that it was a chance as slim as a piece of thread that the 'keeper would have left unused oil in the drum, but he might have left town in a hurry or in despair, uncaring in his haste to make tracks from what had become a ghost town. The clapboard saloon would be tinder-dry. If set alight, it would be a short-lived but roasting inferno that would put legs under Satan himself.

To have his plan work, it would need five things to happen. The pistol load would have to reach the drum with enough spit left in it to pierce it. How much the drum had rusted would play a big part in that. His shooting would have to be accurate, because if Watkins had seen the drum, it would take no time at all for him to cotton on to what he was trying to do, so the most shots he figured he would have before that happened was two. The fourth and very important element in the equation of chance, was the sparks which the bullet penetrating the drum would hopefully generate to ignite the oil. And the most vital condition of all was that the drum would contain oil, and in enough quantity to set the saloon alight.

A lot of ifs and a lot of maybes, which would need a whole lot of luck to overcome.

'I'm waiting, Clooney,' Watkins sang out, cock-a-hoop. 'How long are you going to make me wait?'

'Not long now,' Clooney called back.

The bounty man squeezed the trigger of his sixgun. The first load nicked the drum but buzzed harmlessly away. His second bullet was solidly on target, but failed to penetrate it. Watkins peered over the batwings, the flash in his eyes telling Clooney that he had realized that his seemingly haywire shooting was far from being that.

Watkins pinned Clooney down under a hail of spiteful lead that punctured holes in the rotten shack wall, several of which could have nailed him. Fingers of sunlight poked through the holes in the shack wall inches from where he lay, as a grim reminder of his lucky escape. The empty click of a spent rifle, gave him the opportunity to try for the drum again while Watkins was reloading.

The bullet hitting the drum dead centre had a reassuring solidness. The drum shuddered and quivered and gave a little whining moan. A hair-line crack raced along the drum, like a streak of jagged prairie lightning. Then the crack stopped and held. Frank Clooney's burgeoning hope died. Obviously, the drum's outward decrepitude was a shabbiness rather than an indicator of deep-seated decay. However, just as he gave his mind over to coming up with another plan, if there was another plan, the crack took hold again, racing the length of the drum before becoming a fissure that fractured. Oil began to seep from the fissure. Clooney fired again. A rain-bow of glorious sparks flashed on the drum and danced along the leaking rupture. A flash of orange curled out of the drum, and in a blink it became a raging fireball racing up the tinder-dry wall of the saloon.

Wood crackled.

Old paint blistered.

Waves of sparks and burning embers rolled up the wall, becoming great tongues of fire that curled on to the roof. Leaping sheets of flame, riding on and gaining energy from the hot desert air swept across the roof, while lower down the fire curled round the structure's walls to engulf the front of the building, spreading faster than a saloon whore's legs at the sight of a well-filled

10

wallet. Fire was sucked down through the many holes in the roof, and imploded in the upper floor. The fire leap-frogged to the buildings alongside. Clouds of acrid smoke enveloped the street. Great balls of sparks ignited debris spread far and wide. The town of Good Intentions was in its death throes.

George Watkins danced out of the saloon, brushing glowing embers of debris from his clothing and smouldering hair. But desperate as his plight might be, he was still in a fighting mood.

'Give it up, Watkins,' Frank Clooney advised. 'You're in my sights, and going nowhere but hell.'

'I ain't going to no gallows,' the outlaw bellowed.

He cut loose with a rifle round that was way off the mark, whining harmlessly above the shack, surprisingly inaccurate shooting for a man whose reputation as a *pistolero* was considerable and envied among his peers. Clooney soon spotted the reason for Watkins's lack of lead-slinging proficiency. The back of his right hand was raw from a burn.

A pall of black smoke rolled out of the saloon, which momentarily hid Watkins from the bounty hunter's view. When the smoke rolled away, Watkins was gone. The question for Frank Clooney was, where had he vanished to? The saloon side of the street was by now more or less a raging inferno, so at least that halved the danger, because it only left the ramshackle buildings on the other side as a refuge for Watkins. But even at that, flushing him out would put Clooney in all sorts of danger. It was with relief that he heard the clomp of hoofs. George Watkins, in Clooney's opinion, had chosen the wrong option in trying to flee the town. Had he chosen to hide out, circumstances might have favoured him were Clooney to make a mistake. But galloping along the main street in a headlong dash for freedom was the least sensible thing George Watkins could have done. Watkins had probably figured that hitting a fast-moving target would prove to be a bogie for the bounty hunter.

He was wrong.

CHAPTER ONE

Frank Clooney's horse broke a leg in the most desolate, dangerous and inhospitable stretch of country in which a man could find himself. He cursed his decision to shorten his journey by cutting through a canyon, whose terrain held the risk which had now been his undoing. If it had worked out, he'd have saved a day. Now, stranded, if his luck continued its sour turn the price to pay for trying to gain a day could be the rest of his life.

At the time he had made the decision to divert through the canyon, it had made good sense. But now, with the wisdom of hindsight, it was a decision which made no sense at all. His only hope was to make it to San Gabriel, a slapped-together town that, depending on the day you arrived, might be American or Mexican. Straddling the border, the two countries had laid claim to the ramshackle town which had sprung up in hopes of more gold being found on the strength of one sizeable nugget. Gold and there could be war. No gold, and San Gabriel would be as quickly forgotten as it had been readily disputed. Soon after that, San Gabriel would crumble back into the desert, and would become a curious footnote in history.

He looked up at the canyon's high reaches. The steep rockfaces, acting as reflectors of the scorching sun, sent the temperature of the canyon on a steady upwards climb. The trapped heat made the canyon a cauldron that would, should misfortune befall a man, fry him like a strip of bacon in a hot pan.

Already sensing trouble, vultures were perching on the canyon's rim, expecting the horseless man to be their next feast. Clooney checked his pocket timepiece, a solid-gold watch passed on from generation to generation, smoothened by the many hands which had held it.

Ten thirty a.m.

There was still an hour and a half to noon, when the sun would be directly above the canyon, when it would become as close a place to hell as did not matter.

He cut the mare's throat. A bullet in the head would have been quicker and more humane, but he was in dangerous country, full of dangerous

men, who might want to even a score with the
bounty man who had dispatched or delivered to
the gallows many of their contemporaries or rela-
tives. Gunfire travelled far in the still silence,
maybe to reach the wrong ears. And there were
Indians to consider. Apaches. They had signed a
peace treaty, but not everyone, white or red,
agreed with that treaty. There were renegades on
both sides who were intent on settling old scores.
And the only requirement to settle that score was
that you be white if an Indian was doing the
settling. Or red if a white man had you in his
gunsights.

What really lifted Frank Clooney's skin, was the
fact that as an experienced bounty hunter, who
had tracked a hundred desperadoes in his time,
he should have known better than to think that
he was clever enough to outwit the vagaries of
desert country. It was a golden rule in the desert
not to stray from well-worn trails if you wanted to
enhance your chances of reaching wherever you
were headed. Any diversions added risk to a
man's journey. Nature provided all the risks and
more that a man could handle, and only then if
luck rode with him.

However, his decision to use the canyon to
shorten his journey, though a bad and stupid
decision, was surpassed in both those qualities by
his decision to set free the horse of the man he

had buried ten miles behind him, when the nag's use as a body carrier had ended. In life George Watkins had been rotten, and in death that rotteness had decayed his body faster than another man's, forcing Clooney to bury him before the vultures and a host of other critters lost patience and attacked the living with the dead. The nag had not been up to much, after the years of hard riding and mistreatment by Watkins. He had figured that hauling the beast along behind him would be an impediment he could do without. But right now, had he kept the mare in tow, he would not be stranded. He had been headed to Red Sands to the marshal there to collect his bounty, but his progress had been slowed by the need to take cover a couple of times and outwait the passage of renegade Apaches and an assortment of other evil bastards who would take delight in killing him.

A lot of lawmen liked to see a body before parting with the bounty money, and all would demand some proof of the manhunter's claim. Clooney had taken from Watkins a grisly, well-documented item that should guarantee payment – a diamond ring he had from the last woman he had killed, still on the blackened finger he had cut off, him being in a hurry after raping and murdering her.

The vultures, more of the ugly critters by the

second, looked on, patiently biding their time. They no doubt had gorged themselves on fools before. Angry, he threw a rock at a trio of scavengers who had swooped down for a closer look, uselessly wasting energy which he would need in the not too distant future. A particularly brazen vulture swooped in behind Clooney and ripped a chunk of flesh from the dead mare's hindquarters. Spinning about, Clooney cleared leather and blasted the bird. The Colt's load lifted the foul flesh-forager high into the air. When it came back down among rocks, vultures, being the greedy bastards they were, were feeding on it instantly. Clooney did not bother scattering them. He hoped that with the vulture and the mare to feed on, they would forget about him. At least the feast would give him time, because though vultures were easily dissuaded when a man was full of vigour, they had been known to be less so when a man got weak and helpless through fatigue, thirst and hunger. Then their predatory instincts kicked in, and *as good as dead* was sometimes enough for them to start the feast before the meal was ready.

'Best see if this hellhole of a canyon's got any shelter from the sun,' he murmured.

Alerted by the tearing, sucking sounds, Frank Clooney looked back, his grey eyes filling with disgust. Already the mare's belly was open, and

17

vultures were ripping the horse's innards out. Hardened by years of tough trails ridden and hard men tamed, the bounty hunter still shivered coldly on seeing reflected in the devouring of the mare his own end, if his luck ran out.

And he had instinctively and foolishly used his gun. How many more predators had that alerted?

CHAPTER TWO

Not far into the canyon, the bounty hunter's worries increased. The canyon had myriad offshoots, trails and dead ends. And, more disturbingly, the tracks of unshod ponies.

Indians.

The danger of the honeycomb canyon was the risk of becoming sucked into it, until suddenly the clear-cut route you thought you had followed vanished, and the familiar terrain, in a blink, became an alien landscape from which deliverance would be a matter of luck rather than planning. At first a man would not be too despairing, but as trail after trail, and track after track petered out and his energy was sapped, his brain would begin to boil in the furnace heat. He'd slow, get slower still, his legs becoming weights beyond his capacity to lift. He'd begin to bloat. His lungs would burn. His eyes would bulge. The glaring sun would pass through them to sear his brain. Inevitably, he would drop, and hope that his hell would end quickly. If he was lucky, he would by then be loco.

Clooney stopped to test the freshness of the pony droppings, to get an idea as to how long before they had passed through the canyon. The Apaches had signed a recent Peace Treaty, and in the main were at peace with the white man. However, there were those who disagreed, and saw their chiefs' dealings with the white eyes as treachery. These renegades would have left their villages, and would have to find food and other necessities where they could, and that meant trouble. Not large-scale trouble. But then trouble when it comes knocking on a man's door is always personal. The droppings were powder dry. Fresh droppings meant close-at-hand trouble. Dry droppings meant that the threat was not immediate. At least that was the common wisdom, but the Apaches were smart and cunning. Clooney had heard how the Indians would gather droppings into sacks and age them in the sun. Then they would place them to decieve. A short time later, men who had put their trust in common wisdom, would find the Apaches in their neighbourhood, when it was too late.

A rattler slid past, its rattle clattering. Clooney heeded the snake's warning and gave way.

He had decided to rest by day and travel by
night. Night travel would have its dangers, of
course, but it would have the advantage of cool-
ness. A full moon would help considerably.

His Norwegian/Irish background was working
against him, because he had taken his ma's
colouring, fair hair and fair skin, instead of his
pa's darker Kerry looks. His pa, rest his soul, often
sat him on his knee and told him tales about how
some of the survivors of the defeated Spanish
Armada, unable to make safe passage back to
Spain, had landed in County Kerry.

'Maybe I've got Spanish grandee blood in my
veins, boy,' he would fancifully dream.

Clooney's hide had become leathery from
riding desert trails in his line of business, but not
thick enough to withstand the kind of intense
heat of the barren landscape, horseless and near
waterless. On foot, his punishment would be
multiplied tenfold. Already, behind his right ear
he had the beginnings of a skin ulcer where he
had been bitten by a bug. It had begun to fester,
and would soon fill with pus and become painful.
He'd suffer its discomfort, but hoped that the
infection would remain localized. To keep it so
would not be easy in the fetid heat.

He paused some way into the canyon in his
search for shelter and dropped his saddle. It had
been a stupid idea to shoulder it this far, using up

precious moisture and energy. But it was instinctive for a man to try and save his saddle, as instinctive as holding on to a gun. He had not gone far, but already his back ached from the weight of the saddle. He hid the saddle among boulders, noting a high pointed peak that looked like an accusing finger pointed at heaven to mark the spot, his intention being, if he survived the desert country, to return for the saddle. A saddle was like an old familiar chair. Replace it with a new one and it took a long time to mould the leather to a man's shape and physical oddities.

He unstrapped his canteen from the saddle horn, and took the Winchester from its scabbard. Both items were way below par as effective survival kit. His canteen was only about quarter-full, and the shoot-out with George Watkins had made worrying inroads into his supply of shells for the rifle, should he cross paths with trouble. He had a belt full of bullets for the sixgun hugging his right hip, but for a pistol to be effective a man needed to have not much distance between him and his enemy. Though a finely tooled weapon, the Colt pistol, over a distance, was not an effective deterrent of a determined enemy. To counter a threat before it became an eyeball-to-eyeball encounter, a man needed a rifle with enough shells.

A short distance further into the canyon, and

just when the tracks were beginning to blur one into the other, Clooney spotted a cave, as he thought. But on investigation, after a struggle up a shale path that had him going backwards as often as forward, he saw that *cave* was a grandiose name for what was only a hollow in the rockface, weathered out of the granite by the winds and rains of centuries. But luckily the hollow was deep enough to provide him with shade, though not much protection from the searing heat. The rock of the cocoon gave out waves of debilitating heat. It would be a long day, before the sun would begin its downward slide. He sipped sparingly from his canteen and grimaced. What little water he had was turning sour, and gut sickness became one more concern in a fast-building mountain of worry for Frank Clooney.

CHAPTER THREE

His luck was running bad. Two waterholes which normally would have yielded up a canteen of water, if a man was patient enough to fill it a drop at the time, had proved worthless. One had been completely dried up. And the second had been fouled by the rotting carcass of a coyote. Bad luck in the desert usually meant that the arid land claimed a man.

Clooney's gaze was fixed on a mound of bleached bones not far from where he sat. Near the bones was a discarded and weathered canteen. The canteen had been claimed as home by a colony of ants. The man's skull was home to an army of fat, slow-moving beetles, whose glistening, smooth shell-like backs repulsed Clooney. He shot out his foot and kicked the skull. It rolled down the slope, spilling the beetles from it as it went.

'That'll teach you, you fat, slimy bastards!' he swore.

But he could not help thinking that, maybe, the insects would have the last laugh by making their home inside his bleached skull.

The day dragged on into evening, and a breeze that often follows the intense heat of the day in the desert began to blow. Clooney welcomed its soothing balm. Night crept into the canyon, its long fingers reaching into every nook and cranny, like a ghostly thief searching for the treasure men might have hidden during the day. There wasn't anything in the way of kindling to start a fire, so Clooney had to be satisfied with jerky and cold beans. His belly still hollow, he began to walk in what he hoped was the right direction for San Gabriel. He knew the country reasonably well, but he also knew the trickery of the desert. What seemed familiar became suddenly unfamiliar and a man became hopelessly lost. It had been some time since he had last visited San Gabriel, and he hoped that he would not find a mountain of dust and nothing more.

It was a town born out of a gold strike, and its transient nature had been reflected in its ramshackle and tossed-together buildings, investment limited until the lode was proved to be worthwhile and longer term profits to replace the quick-buck fever were a real prospect. San

Gabriel would exist only until the vein ran out, unless wisdom prevailed and a share of the proceeds from the strike was invested in land reclamation, good water and sanitation. Some goldrush hamlets survived to become viable towns where post gold-fever businesses such as cattle and commerce took over to provide a living for those not of a mind to follow the latest gold-strike rumour. But mostly they remained tent-and-shack towns thrown together by the providers of pleasure, whose only interest was in fleecing the miners who would leave town with pockets as empty as when they had arrived, and with only their dreams of the next El Dorado to comfort them.

The bounty hunter recalled that on a previous visit to San Gabriel the town had had the signs of roots being put down. Among the tents and shacks there was the lumber for more permanent structures to replace them, harvested from the hills to the south of town. But by now those hills could be stripped bare in the hunt for gold, timber not as important to the gold-fevered as it was to potential settlers. And without the essential resource of lumber for building, no town could rise from the barren plains, despite the best efforts of good men.

San Gabriel had had a good well, with a hope of a second equally productive well in prospect.

But with the best will in the world, if Mexico had finally claimed the town, the Yanquis would not be popular or welcome. Nor indeed would the *Americanos* wish to remain under Mex rule, which at best was tyrannical, and at worst cruel and barbaric.

By now, if the town had folded, the well would probably be fouled or would have caved in. But then again, maybe it had not. He'd soon find out. Anyway, he did not have a choice. Without a horse, San Gabriel was the nearest refuge he could reach.

The desert night was cold, and as bad luck would have it, cloudy. The pressure of a storm had been building all afternoon. It had veered off south and that was a blessing, but it had left in its wake a trail of cloud that raced across the moon, creating a patchwork of light and shadow that added to the dangers of passage. Watching eyes glowed in the dark, sizing up a prospective meal. Clooney had no idea what kind of critters the eyes belonged to. All he could hope for was that they belonged to an animal small enough to be more frightened than he was. Or if they were the eyes of a more predatory enemy, that it had eaten well and would be too lazy to bother with another meal. He picked his steps carefully, his progress of necessity slow. An injury was the last thing he needed. He also had to be careful that once the heat of a new day started to build he would be near shelter, and that need gave him a dilemma. Because each possible hidy-hole he came to and passed, might be the very one at which he'd regret not having ended the first leg of his trek.

Not far from first light, and pleased with the progress he had made, Clooney heard the snort of a horse beyond a rise, and picked up the smell of woodsmoke.

Apaches, was his first and terrifying thought.

He grabbed handfuls of dirt and rubbed the grit into the crown and brim of his relatively new hat, purchased with some of the proceeds of his last bounty payment. That done, he rubbed the dirt into his face, until only his eyes showed. Clean hats and shiny faces tended to catch a man's eyes. All that was needed after that to get a bullet between the eyes was a nervous trigger finger. Then, measuring each step, he crept up the rise, crouched as low as he could.

Nearing the top, he belly-crawled to the edge of the rise and peered over into the hollow below. A man was sitting near the dying embers of a fire, his back against the stump of a tree, an empty whiskey bottle on the ground beside him. He mumbled incoherently. Clooney could not be certain of the man's mutterings, but from what he could catch it sounded like the man was replaying in his mind a game of poker. Some men dreamed of women. Some men dreamed of cards. Others dreamed of lush range filled with cows. In the cruel West, all men dreamed of something.

Clooney's gaze went to the wagon at the far side of the hollow. The wagon's team resting nearby seemed to be in good shape, as did the wagon. The water barrel on the side of the rig caught his eye, and his tongue, as dry as the desert brush, licked lips that were even drier still. Frank Clooney could not believe his luck. His urge was to barrel straight into the hollow, but he reined in his enthusiasm. The rifle propped against the man's right shoulder was a positive disincentive to rash behaviour. Disturbed, the sleeping man might react in a shoot-first-ask-questions-later manner. As the man was in a drunken sleep, the risk of that happening was low, but why take a risk at all? If he was forced to draw iron on the man, it would not be the best start to their meeting, and it would likely scupper any chance of hitching a ride.

He'd wait. Let the man wake. Give him time to gather his wits. Besides, he did not know who might be sleeping in the wagon, or be bunked down among the boulders. Some men risked bunking down in boulders to gain the comfort of the heat which the rock absorbed during the day and released through the chilly desert night. His preference would be to not risk lying down with any one of a hundred critters who could make a man's sleep permanent. The man might be alone, but Frank Clooney doubted it. He had obviously felt secure enough to get drunk, and that probably meant, unless the man was an utter fool or a victim of liquor-fever, that someone else with shooting skills was on hand should danger threaten.

Clooney settled down to wait.

'Emily, are you awake?'

Clooney started. A woman's voice. Well spoken. Educated. He again crawled to the edge of the rise. His pulse quickened on seeing the shapely form of a woman on the canvas of the wagon, illuminated by the glow of a lamp.

'Emily,' the woman complained. 'Time to be up.'

The smaller form of a young girl joined the woman.

Too late, Clooney noiced the absence of the sleeping man. He felt the cold prod of a rifle on the back of his head.

'Twitch and I'll blow it clean off your shoulders, mister,' was the man's icy warning.

CHAPTER FOUR

'Quench that damn lamp, Becca!' the man bellowed. 'Less'n you want to be seen by a stranger's eyes, that is.'

The light of the lamp instantly vanished.

'Now, mister,' the man said, not a hint of compromise in his voice. 'You've got explainin' to do. And it better be good explainin' at that.' The rifle prodded Clooney. 'Up. Slow. Real slow,' he cautioned as the bounty hunter obliged. 'Hands tippin' the sky, fella.' The man relieved Clooney of his rifle and sixgun. 'Don't like my woman to be watched,' he growled, ramming the barrel of his rifle between Clooney's shoulders.

Clooney knew that he was living life by the second.

'Git on down there,' the man ordered, 'and no tricks. This 'chester's trigger would react to a man's breath blowed on it.'

Clooney cursed his complacency. He had fallen for a very old trick. A man with an empty bottle feigning drunkenness.

'Must be getting old,' he murmured, making his way down into the hollow.

His captor grunted.

'Wouldn't worry, mister,' he said. 'You ain't got much time left an'way.'

The woman dropping to the ground from the wagon, whose lamplit form had promised so much, did not disappoint in reality. She was busily putting her waistlength mane of midnight-black hair in a bun. Her intelligent blue eyes were on Clooney, scrutinizing every inch of him.

'Caught me a peeper, Becca,' the man growled. This time it was the butt of the rifle instead of the barrel which he rammed between Clooney's shoulders. Clooney grimaced, but refused to go down under the crunching blow. But when two further blows rained in, the choice was not his. He dropped to his knees. The man's boot quickly followed through and Frank Clooney curled up in a ball.

'Damn peeper!' he roared.

'Take it easy, Ned,' the woman called Becca said.

'Easy?' Ned whined. 'Are you pleadin' for this bastard, Becca?'

'No,' she said hastily, flinching as the man she

had addressed as Ned leaned threateningly towards her.

'Seems t' me like you is, woman!' he growled.

Worriedly, the young girl poking her head between the wagon flaps asked: 'You OK, Ma?'

'Get back inside, you brat,' Ned barked. 'Or I'll lay your back bare with a whip.' Terrified, the girl withdrew back into the wagon. 'Get a rope,' he instructed the woman. 'I'm goin' to wagon haul this bastard right now.'

'There was no real harm done, Ned,' Becca said.

'No harm done,' he yelled. 'That's 'cause I got the drop on him, woman.'

'Can't you see that he's all in,' she said.

'That about sums it up, ma'am,' Clooney said. 'My horse broke a leg yesterday. I've been walking all night.'

Ned scowled. 'Walkin' to where?'

'San Gabriel, about twenty miles east of here. Maybe you're headed that way yourselves?'

'Maybe,' Ned said slyly. 'Depends.'

'On what?' Clooney asked, already knowing the answer.

'On what you got to buy passage with, o' course.' Ned grunted. 'And it would have to be good, too. 'Cause we was headed to Red Sands, the only proper town in this neck o' the woods.'

'Red Sands, huh,' Frank Clooney said. 'That's

fifty miles or more through country that's hotter than hell's hob. Indian country, too.'

'The Apache is all washed up,' Ned snorted. 'Don't agree with no treaty with them savages though. Should be wiped out, I say. Ev'ry last one.'

'A treaty is good, Ned,' Becca opined. 'Now folk will be able to homestead and ranch in peace.'

In a sudden burst of anger, Ned back-handed the woman.

'If'n I want your opinion I'll ask for it,' he raged. ' 'Paches ain't no better than the turd in my ass, you hear.' His rage vanished as quickly as it had manifested itself. He chuckled. 'A woman is best silent unless she's under a man,' he told Clooney.

Frank Clooney seethed at the man's treatment of the woman, but he was stranded in the desert, so his first priority was to hitch a ride before thirst and exhaustion would leave his bones bleaching.

The young girl leapt from the wagon and lunged tigerishly at the man, but her hammering fists might as well have been beating on rock for all the effect they had on the apish Ned. Tiring of the girl's futile battle, he contemptuously tossed her aside.

'What kind of man are you?' Emily Carver screamed at Clooney.

'A man who minds his own business, miss,' the bounty hunter answered in an offhand manner. 'A man's chastisement of his kin ain't none of my affair.'

'Sensible fella,' was Ned's opinion. 'Leave the brat,' he ordered Becca, when she went to comfort the distraught girl. He grabbed her by the hair and shoved her towards the wagon. 'Hitch up the team.'

'I'm fine, Ma,' Emily said, bouncing back to her feet, relieving Becca of having to defy the bully.

'What about breakfast?' Becca asked.

'Ain't got no time for no breakfast, woman.'

'Why not, Ned? We're not going anywhere that needs hurrying to.'

Clooney admired the woman's spirit. And it was that same spirit, he guessed, that riled the bully she was travelling with. Her husband? An unlikely match if ever he'd seen one. There was no doubting but that the girl was hers, there wasn't a smidgen of the man anywhere in her.

Ned started towards the woman, hand raised to swipe at her.

'I warned you not to give me any sass, woman,' he fumed.

'You leave my ma be,' the girl screamed.

'You mind your own business, Emily,' Becca rebuked her, looping her arm through Ned's. 'My man knows what's best for me, and you too. Isn't that so, honey?'

'Ma,' the young girl said, disgusted by Becca's fawning, not understanding that the purpose of sidling up to Ned was to save her from harm.

'And you listen to your pa, young lady,' Becca rebuked Emily, even more sternly. 'And do as he tells you to.'

'He ain't my pa!'

'Ned's my man. So that makes him your pa, you hear.'

Weeping bitterly, the girl ran back to the wagon.

Ned laughed brutishly. He pulled the woman to him and kissed her hard, letting his hands wander where they might. The woman's pleading eyes locked with Frank Clooney's, and their message was clear. Any intervention by him would only make matters worse. And the need to convey that message meant that she had seen or sensed the concern behind his charade of unconcern in Ned's brutality towards her and Emily.

'You know,' Ned said to the woman. 'I reckon we've got time for breakfast after all, and maybe even a little more.'

'Anything you say or want, honey,' Becca said, fawning even more.

'Now what'm I goin' to do with you, mister?' Ned pondered.

'Oh, he's not important, Ned,' Becca said, cuddling closer to him. 'Let him be.'

'Is that what you want, darlin'?' he asked.

'It's not what *I* want, Ned, honey,' she stressed. 'It's just that riff-raff like him just isn't worth you wasting your energy on.'

'Guess he ain't at that,' Ned concurred. 'Git,' he ordered Clooney.

'You'd send a man back into the desert,' Clooney challenged. 'To certain death?'

'Want that I should shoot you right here and now?' Ned growled. 'It'd be m' pleasure, fella.'

Becca put her hand on the pointed rifle, and suggestively stroked its barrel. Ned swallowed hard.

'The sound of gunfire travels far in the desert, Ned,' she said. 'And no one can tell whose ears it will reach.'

'Smart woman,' he said to Clooney. 'But,' he drew a sheathed hunting-knife from his boot, 'there's quiet ways to kill a man, too.'

'Don't waste your time with a weasel, honey.' Becca slid her arm possessively round Ned's waist. 'He's not worth the bother.' She strode over to Clooney and spat in his face, much to Ned's amusement.

Frank Clooney wiped the spittle from his cheek and, playing the role the woman clearly wanted him to play, cringed and whimpered.

'You're right, honey,' Ned said, pulling Becca to him. 'He ain't worth killin'. Git!' He again repeated. ' 'Fore I change m' mind.'

Whimpering, Clooney said: 'I need to hitch a ride real bad, mister.'

The man called Ned glared at the bounty hunter. 'Ain't got no room. 'Sides, I don't want the company of no coward.'

Becca exchanged a flashing glance with Clooney.

'Maybe, like you said, he can pay his way, Ned,' she said. 'We could use the money.'

Ned pondered some. Then: 'You got money, fella?'

'Yeah. Some.'

'How much exactly is some?' The eager question was Becca's.

'Twenty dollars,' Clooney answered.

The woman snorted. 'Not much, is it.'

'Turn out your pockets,' Ned ordered Clooney. The bounty hunter cowered, postured and snivelled as he reckoned a coward would. 'Turn 'em out,' Ned growled, threateningly raising the rifle butt. 'Or I'll bust your skull open and turn 'em out m'self.'

Clooney drew back as a mistreated dog might.

'Sure, mister,' he whined.

'Hand it over,' Ned said, when Clooney had searched all of his pockets. He quickly counted the bills. 'Damn liar,' he roared. 'There's thirty dollars here.'

Puttting up his hands to ward off the expected blow, Clooney whimpered:

'Sorry, mister. You ain't going to beat me, are you?'

'You deserve nothing less than a good whipping,' Becca said with fake anger, and quickly added before Ned took her opinion as a licence to lay in to Clooney, 'But like I said, it isn't worth my man wasting his energy on a whiner like you.'

'We got thirty dollars we didn't have,' Ned laughed. 'So let's hitch up the team and roll, Becca.' Clooney went to follow. 'And where d'ya think you're goin'?' he growled.

Clooney looked bemused.

'Like I said,' Ned growled, 'I don't want no coward for company.'

Frank Clooney looked to Becca for help. She shrugged impassively. 'Ned's the boss, mister. What he says, goes.'

They strolled off, Ned to hitch up the team, and Becca to pack up their belongings. Clooney waited, hoping that he had not misjudged or misinterpreted the woman's intentions. If he had, his predicament had worsened considerably. Now he was horseless, waterless and skint. If he happened on a horse trader who frequented the desert to trade with outlaws and unfortunates who needed fresh horseflesh, thirty dollars might have bought him a nag of sorts, depending on how brisk the trader's business was.

With the wagon ready to roll, Frank Clooney reckoned he had been the fool of all fools to have trusted the woman. It looked like she was no better than the man she was with, though he would have sworn on a stack of Bibles that she was several cuts above him. Not that that would be hard, with him being so low down the scale of human kind.

'You can't leave him here,' the girl pleaded. 'He'll surely die.'

'So let him die,' Becca said, uncaringly.

'You're no better than he is, Ma,' the girl railed contemptuously, and vanished back inside the wagon.

The woman leaned across the wagon seat to whisper to Ned, her eyes darting back to Clooney. Her whispering perked up the man's interest in Clooney. He shook his head doubtfully. The woman whispered some more. Ned considered. Then:

'I guess the kid is right,' he called to Clooney. 'Me being a Christian soul, it wouldn't be right to let you to perish in this heathen country.'

'Thanks.'

Clooney scampered eagerly to the wagon.

Frank Clooney did not know what Becca had

40

whispered to Ned, but of one thing he was now certain, he had not misread her.

'Name's Carver,' Ned said. 'And this fine woman is m' wife. And the snot-nosed brat you're sharin' the wagon with is m' daughter Em'ly.'

'I ain't your kid!' Emily spat. 'My pa's dead.'

'Now, Emily,' Becca scolded the girl. 'We've been through all of this a hundred times. Ned is your pa now. So you show him respect, girl.'

'Never!' Emily groused sullenly.

'We've got a guest on board now,' Becca said, 'so you've got to be obedient and mannerly. We don't want Mr. . . ?'

'Rafter, ma'am,' Clooney lied. 'Sam Rafter.'

Using his own name might not be the wisest thing to do, he had decided. He had quite a rep as a bounty hunter, and he figured that in the company Ned Carver would keep, his name might have come up for mention. Bounty men were about as welcome as the plague, and were he to be revealed as such, any chance of hitching a ride would probably be gone. Best to keep his real identity secret. That way he would also keep his edge. He was in the company of a viper who could decide to bite at any time along the trail.

'Mr Rafter, Emily,' Becca continued, 'to get the wrong impression.'

Ned Carver shook with laughter.

'Becca, honey,' he said. 'I reckon Mr Rafter's

41

impressions are already formed.'

He cracked the whip over the team and the wagon rolled, on the beginning of what Frank Clooney reckoned would be Hell's trail.

CHAPTER FIVE

The morning wore on, the heat relentlessly building. Ned Carver's mood soured more with each degree of heat that was added, and by noon his mood was black and brooding. All the while Becca Carver became edgier, until her back and shoulders were rigid to the point of brittleness. Like her mother, Emily Carver's tension grew steadily. It did not surprise Frank Clooney any when the trapping of the wagon's left-sided rear wheel in a sandy pocket at the edge of the trail, was the spark that ignited the powder keg that was Ned Carver's anger.

'Honey,' Becca pleaded, when Carver began to mindlessly flay the horses with his whip, taking revenge on the hapless nags for his own carelessness in allowing the wagon to deviate from the solid narrow strip in the centre of the track that could be relied on to safely bear the wagon's weight. 'It ain't the horses fault.'

'That so. You sayin' that it's my fault, woman?' he raged.

'No, I'm not, Ned.' Becca Carver flinched and tensed as her husband shifted in his seat, telling Clooney that she expected Carver to strike out. Becca's anticipation of violence was evidence of its frequency and cruelty. 'Wagons bog down all the time, honey. We can easily get it back on track.' She glanced back into the wagon. 'Mr Rafter will help, won't you?'

'Sure will, ma'am,' came Frank Clooney's willing reply.

'Don't you look at him that way!' Carver fumed. 'Like you wanted to . . .' He raised his arm, the back of his hand ready to swipe out at Becca. 'Just don't you look at him that way, woman.'

Emily leapt up and clawed at Carver.

'You leave my ma be, you no-good.'

Carver swung about in the wagon seat and used the hand he had threatened Becca with on Emily. The force of the blow catapulted the girl backwards, and were it not for Clooney's swift reaction, the blow would have knocked the girl clean out of the wagon. Becca screamed. Carver dragged her back, when she tried to go to Emily's assistance.

'Let the brat whine all she damn well likes.' He

held Becca fast to the wagon seat. 'And you stay put, if you don't want the same.'

'I'm OK, Ma,' Emily wept. 'He can't hurt me none.'

Becca Carver wept with her daughter.

'Shuddup!' Ned Carver roared. 'Damn whinin' skirts!'

'How can you just sit there? you being a man and all, and do nothing,' Emily accused Clooney. Emily pushed him away. 'Guess that makes you no better than him.'

'Interfere an' I'll kill ya!' Carver threatened the bounty hunter.

Frank Clooney shrugged. 'Ain't none of my affair, Carver. They're your women. You chastise them as you see fit.'

Ned Carver grunted. 'Wise fella,' he said, and warned: 'You just be sure to keep thinkin' like that, and there'll be no problems.'

'Like I said,' Clooney repeated with an even greater lack of interest, 'your women, your business.'

'Pig!' Emily Carver screamed at Clooney.

'You show respect to our guest, brat,' Carver growled, obviously now reckoning on Frank Clooney as an ally. 'Or I'll whip you senseless, girl.' He rooted under the wagon seat and came up with a bottle of rotgut. Using his rotten teeth, he uncorked the bottle and swigged liberally from it. When he offered the bottle to Clooney, there was quarter of it clear glass. Carver belched loudly and uninhibitedly broke wind. 'Slug 'fore we get to work on diggin' that damn wheel out.'

'Don't mind if I do.'

Clooney, though not really a whiskey-drinking man, drank deeply, matching Carver's consumption because he would have expected nothing less now that they were, in Carver's mind, *compadres*. When he handed the bottle back, there was half of it clear glass. Ned Carver nodded his approval.

'You,' Carver's eyes included Becca and Emily, 'unload the wagon to make it lighter.' He jumped down and sat on a boulder. Playing his role to the hilt, Frank Clooney joined him to watch Becca and Emily labour in the intense heat. While outwardly the bounty hunter shared in Carver's cruel amusement, inwardly he raged at the woman and girl's inhuman treatment. But, horseless and gunless, Carver having grabbed his rifle and .45, there was nothing he could do. If he acted on his righteous anger, Carver would hold sway. Should that happen it would serve no good purpose. Carver would kill him or leave him to die, and Becca and Emily Carver would still suffer his monstrous cruelty. He'd bide his time until an opportunity presented itself, but it would not be easy to suffer Becca and Emily's humiliation, or the girl's look of utter contempt. Becca Carver, he hoped, would be able to reason out the need for patience. He was convinced now that her whisperings to Ned Carver, which had changed his mind about having him along, had been to make his inclusion possible in the hope that her and Emily's plight would be resolved. An intelligent woman, she had to know that there was only one way that that could be done, and that was by killing Ned Carver.

There was no good reason why he should be, but Frank Clooney was disappointed in the fact that, obviously, Becca Carver saw in him a potential killer. Had the long years of bounty hunting given him an aura that Becca Carver sensed? He had once heard an older bounty man say that death, even justified death, clung to a man.

'Seeps into him,' he'd said.

And the only way to cleanse it was to hang up his gun.

'When you do that,' the older bounty man had told Clooney, 'the shadow of the Grim Reaper riding with you passes to the next man who'll do his bidding.'

At the telling, round a camp-fire they had shared, Frank Clooney had dismissed his fellow bounty hunter's ramblings as loco talk. Now he wasn't at all sure.

'Most of the stuff's out, Ned,' Becca said. 'A couple of trunks that are too heavy to lift are all that's left.'

'Finish it,' Carver snarled, again offering the bottle of rotgut to Clooney. He scoffed. 'Liftin' strengthens the backbone.'

'Obliged, friend,' Clooney said, downing what remained of the whiskey.

Not being as hard-guzzling a man as Carver, Frank Clooney felt a wobble in his legs when he joined him in scraping out a hole and filling it with shale to provide the snagged wagon wheel with a grip. Greatly amused, Carver did an impression of Clooney's wobbling gait.

Packing the last of the shale under the wheel, Carver said in a leery aside:

'Sluggin' whiskey makes me kinda lovin', if you get m' drift, partner.'

'I reckon I do at that,' Clooney replied, winking.

'When this wagon wheel's back on solid ground, you can have the girl if you want.'

Frank Clooney had to work hard to hide his shock and rage. And even harder still to keep his smile fixed.

'Later, mebbe,' he said, careful not to work up Carver's wrath by an outright refusal of his offer. He winked. 'Whiskey kills in one man what it brings to life in another.'

'Hear tell that that's so.' Carver lewdly grabbed his crotch and sniggered. 'Hard to believe though. Let's get this damn wheel free, pronto. He called to Becca, 'Get on board, woman. And don't you spare that whip.' Clooney added his shoulder to Carver's and the wheel spun free of its trap. Carver, his face contorted with lust, instructed the bounty hunter, 'Keep the brat outta the wagon, 'til I'm done.'

He strode ahead and swung on to the wagon.

'Git in the back,' he ordered Becca. Frank Clooney did not hear Becca Carver's whispered response, but the sound of Ned Carver's slap rang clear. 'Now git in the back of the damn wagon!'

Emily was on her way to the wagon when Clooney grabbed her. She fought him tigerishly. Emily wept bitterly when the wagon's movement told its story, and Becca cried out. The bounty hunter had killed a lot of men, all of whom had deserved to die. But for him, at that moment, none more so than Ned Carver.

CHAPTER SIX

'Howdy.'

Frank Clooney swung around on hearing the man's greeting. The rider, a bony specimen, sat his saddle in a peculiar, lopsided fashion. Clooney knew the reason for his unorthodox saddle gait. It came from an old knife-wound that had healed badly, and the bunched flesh of the wound made it difficult for the man to ride straight in the saddle for any long period; therefore over time he had developed a style of riding from which, on seeing him approach, one would expect him to topple from his nag at any second. The last time Clooney had crossed paths with Spitter Larch, a nickname earned by his continuous spitting out of tobacco shreds from the quirly that almost never left his lips, had been in a cantina in Nogales, the kind of dive where, if a fella did not catch the pox from a whore, he'd catch something equally deadly but quicker from the latrine water that passed as beer or the swill that was served up as food. Larch was dragging deeply on a quirly now. He was a man passionately addicted to the weed. He would remain so right to the end which, if lead poisoning did not get him first, could not be that far off if the gaunt visage he presented was an indicator of his well-being. Men joked that when Spitter Larch finally met the devil, his first request would be for a pouch of tobacco and a match by way of reward for services rendered.

'You've got a real hellcat on your hands there, mister,' Larch observed.

Because Emily had been weeping quietly for the last couple of minutes, the fight gone out of her, Larch's observation told Frank Clooney that he had been watching, but for how long? Larch, though a cold-blooded killer, was not a man who acted hastily. He had a reputation as a careful man, so Clooney could count on Larch having pretty well sized up the situation before putting in an appearance.

'Trouble?' Larch enquired of Emily.

'Nothing I can't handle,' Emily Carver said, defiantly wiping away her tears and stalking off.

Clooney knew that Larch's concern was not for the girl; his query was made solely to satisfy his curiosity and foster his self-interest. There just might be an angle he could work to make himself a dollar. Clooney knew Larch to be a man completely devoid of any motivation other than his own comfort. Any threat to that, and he'd kill a man, woman or child without qualm.

'No trouble,' Clooney said.

'Your kid?' Larch enquired.

'No. But I reckon that you already know that.'

Spitter Larch smiled with about as much warmth as a rattler before spitting.

'I might say that you ain't a very friendly sorta fella,' he told Clooney.

'And I might say that you're a mighty inquisitive *hombre*,' Clooney retorted.

'And I might add that you're welcome to each other,' Emily Carver spat, obviously having made up her mind, and correctly so, that Spitter Larch's humanitarian concern was about as worthless as a holed water-bucket.

Larch's hollow laugh brought on a spasm of coughing that left him gasping for breath and hanging on to his saddle horn for support. Blood, dark and mucuous-laden, stained his lips, and his hawkish face, despite the leathery bronzing which long stays in desert country had given his skin, took on a pallor that told of tubercular or tumoured lungs.

'A sassy filly,' was Larch's opinion when he got enough breath back to speak.

'Yeah,' Frank Clooney agreed. 'Sass ain't something she's short on.'

The note of admiration in Clooney's tone had Emily Carver looking at him with a new interest. A loud, animal-like groan from the wagon brought a rush of tears to her eyes, and diverted Spitter Larch's attention to the wagon.

'Sounds like a well satisfied fella, don't he?' Larch said. As he glanced at Emily, the killer's eyes reflected his thoughts.

Seconds later, Ned Carver appeared pulling up his trousers with one hand, unashamed of his flagging erection. In the other hand he held a rifle.

'Who're you?' he demanded of Larch.

Clooney took Emily aside, out of the path of any flying lead.

Unmoved, unimpressed and unthreatened, Larch said:

'The last man who held a gun on me ain't 'round no more. Neither are the fellas who tried before him.' Larch sneered. 'Are you planning on joining them, mister?'

Ned Carver's laughter was a show of bravado, but there was no denying the tremble in his laughter as it faded under Spitter Larch's fearsome gaze.

'I gotta rifle ready and pointin', mister,' he said. 'You'd want to be the fastest draw I ever seen to beat the odds you're facin'.'

'I'll kill you for sure in the next coupla seconds if you keep pointing that 'chester at me,' Larch intoned. 'And I am the fastest draw there is,' he added.

Frank Clooney could have told Carver that if it came to gunplay, Larch would be as good as his word. The last Wanted poster for Larch had a figure of $3,000 for his capture dead or alive. He was wanted for every crime in the book, and for some that had not yet been included because no man reckoned that another man could be so evil to commit them. But $3,000 was still not enough for any bounty hunter to risk going after Larch. Not since he had sent the head of the last one who had tried back to his woman. If Carver persisted with his challenge, he'd be a dead man. That, Clooney figured, might not be a bad thing. The world could well do without Ned Carver. But, were Larch to kill him, it would simply be a case of the devil himself taking the place of his disciple.

'You do just that, mister,' Emily Carver prompted Larch. 'If any man does, Ned Carver deserves killing.'

'Have you got anything to say in this matter?' Larch quizzed Clooney.

'Tell him to kill Carver,' Emily urged the bounty hunter.

Frank Clooney grinned lazily. 'I learned a long time ago to not take sides, friend,' he told Larch.

Larch chuckled. 'Likely then that you'll live to be an old man,' he opined.

'That's my aim, sure enough,' Clooney said.

The outlaw returned his gaze to Ned Carver, delivering a chilly ultimatum. 'Drop the 'chester or use it. Or I'll kill you just for your impudence.'

The awareness that had been building in Ned Carver of having bitten off way more than he could chew sent shivers through him. Being a man without even a smidgen of pride, backing down posed no dilemma for him.

'Only tomfoolin', friend,' he said, grovelling. 'You can take a joke, can't ya?'

'Are you calling me a sourpuss?' Larch challenged, reluctant to let go of a killing opportunity, once he had been presented with one. Because Larch was a man who got a peculiar feeling in his groin when he killed another man, which over time had become as addictive as his taste for the weed he constantly puffed. 'Well, are you?' he growled.

'Shucks, no,' Carver prattled. 'No offence, mis—'

'Shut up!' Larch snarled.

'Yes, sir. Sure, mister.' A greasy sweat seeped from Ned Carver's pores, but the killer had lost interest in him. Larch's gaze was fixed on Becca

Carver coming from the wagon with a fiery intensity. 'This here is my wife, Becca. Real fine woman, ain't she.' The sly sparkle in the glance he exchanged with Larch spoke of his willingness to trade Becca, should that be to his advantage.

Becca Carver shivered, the desert heat not enough to ward off the chill in her blood at what Ned Carver was implying with his knowing glance.

'Ain't you a man at all?' Emily Carver fierily accused Frank Clooney.

Emily's scorn made him cringe and wrinkle up inside. And mighty guilty, too, that he had put his own needs before Emily and Becca Carver's welfare. Some men should be chastised, and Carver was such a man. His laxity and self-interest had now presented him with a double problem. Because Larch was quickly discovering that in Ned Carver he had found a man with a soul every modicum as black as his own.

Larch had dismounted, and Carver had sidled up to the outlaw to talk to him in an undertone, his eyes flitting back and forth to Becca, while all the time the sexual tension in Larch mounted, as did Becca Carver's apprehension in proportion. Carver completed muttering with Larch.

'You're surely welcome to tag 'long with us, Mr Larch,' he announced generously.

'That's all we need,' Emily Carver rasped. 'Another snake!'

'You keep the brat's lip buttoned,' Carver roared at Becca. He started towards Emily, sliding the belt from his trousers. 'Or I'll damn well button it for her.'

Becca stood between Carver and Emily to shield the girl from his onslaught.

'I'm not afraid, Ma,' Emily said, spiritedly defiant.

The veins on Ned Carver's face bulged with anger. He curled the belt around his right hand, ready to flay Emily.

'I've taken enough damn nonsense from the brat,' he raged.

Against his better judgement, Frank Clooney stepped forward to block Carver's bullish rush towards Becca and Emily.

'Git outta m' way,' Carver bellowed.

The bounty hunter stood firm. 'Whupping kids isn't man's work, Carver,' he growled.

Ned Carver's gimlet eyes locked with the bounty hunter's unfazed gaze. He glowered.

'You figgerin' on stoppin' me, Rafter? That would be a mighty unwise move to make.'

Frank Clooney cursed silently. His rash action had sharpened Spitter Larch's interest in him anew, at a time when a low profile instead of a challenging persona would have been the safer and less conspicuous option.

Clooney dropped his head to shade it as best

he could with the brim of his Stetson. But so intense had Larch's scrutiny become that he feared that Larch's memory, prompted, would take him back to a cantina in Nogales.

Sitting on Hell's hob would have been cooler than that Mexican day two years previously. It had been the kind of energy-sapping day that boiled a man's brain in his skull and made him mean. The woman, though a whore, had exercised her right to refuse a hardcase in tow with Spitter Larch. At first he had taken the woman's refusal as a negotiating ploy to dig deeper into his pocket, or perhaps as teasing foreplay. She would know that holding out only stoked a man's lust all the more. But when it became clear that her refusal was not a tactic, the man's mood, as ugly as a cancer, became uglier still. He struck her full-fisted in the belly. The woman curled up on the floor, moaning. The hardcase stalked back to rejoin the poker-game he had bowed out of, when the woman had entered the cantina with an empty bucket from which she had fed swill to the pigs out back of the cantina.

'Are you going to let a whore tell you no?' Larch had taunted him, when his interest in the woman had passed its peak.

'No, I damn well ain't!' the man fumed, in response to Larch's taunt.

He grabbed the moaning woman by her long mane of midnight-black hair, and dragged her screaming along the floor to the stinking back room which the cantina made available for the lucrative trade of satisfying men's lust.

'Bet you ain't going to make her moan like that when you're pleasuring her,' Spitter Larch sniggered.

The hardcases round the gambling-table laughed. Other men who were not of Larch's bunch laughed also, when the killer's eyes swept their way. No one with a smidgen of sense bucked Larch, except a fella who saw no point in living longer than the second in which he was sucking air. Therefore, when a steel-trimmed voice spoke, each man in the cantina sought out the fool or loco man in their midst.

'The lady said no, fella.'

His words of that day now rushed back to haunt Frank Clooney. Then, as now, he had acted impulsively when he should have known that impetuosity in the lawless land he traversed was a trait that had made many men wormbait.

'Yeah,' the hardcase had sneered. 'Are you puttin' yourself forward as this whore's protector, mister?'

'You've had your fun,' Clooney intoned. 'The lady said no, now let her be.'

The hardcase sneered. 'It's 'cause I ain't had

no fun yet that's made me mean, mister.' His eyes narrowed to slits. 'Meaner than a sidewinder!'

Spitter Larch temporarily folded his cards, finding Clooney's challenge of his sidekick of more interest for the time being.

'Kill him and be done with it, Larry,' said a tequila-swiller propping up the bar. 'A man can't take no lip from a saloon whore.' The man's drunken gaze settled on Clooney. 'Nor from no nose-pokin' bastard interferin' with your pleasure neither.'

'I guess Hank's about got it right, mister,' the hardcase called Larry told Frank Clooney, settling his gun on his right hip.

'You can try,' was the bounty hunter's steely-eyed response, 'but I'd think about it. Because I'll sure as hell kill you, fella.'

The whore-beater's cocky grin slipped and curled away to hide at the corners of his mouth, while he sized up the stranger who had dared to even think of such a threat, let alone voice it. Finding more mettle in him than he had expected, Larry Ganz being used to putting fast legs under former challengers if he was feeling generous on the day, which was seldom, he felt a finger of ice trickle along his spine. His challenger's slight shift of stance might have gone unnoticed by a less well-versed troublemaker, but Ganz recognized it for what it was – the taking up of a gun-drawing stance.

Normally Ganz, being a *pistolero* of repute, would not be worried, because a long blood-soaked trail had proved him to be more than a match for any man of a mind to draw iron on him. But now, facing a man unafraid and of an unflinching nature was something new to the gunnie. His gut feeling was that should he choose to draw on the stranger, it would be the last thing he'd do this side of hell. But a man of Larry Ganz's lack of intelligence did not have the wit to find a way out of his dilemma.

'What're you waitin' for, Ganz?' the drunk prodded.

Ganz!

The name was synonomous with a fast gun and no mercy. Clooney let no hint of the uncertainty he was now feeling show on his granite-hard features. He was fast, but as fast as Larry Ganz? There were signs that Ganz was desperately looking for a way out but, Clooney thought morbidly, losing face for a man of Ganz's reputation and bone-headedness would probably be worse than dying. Because with his fearsome reputation as an ace gunslinger in tatters, he would be a man of no standing and no respect, even if that respect was the shallow respect of fear and intimidation.

'Shuddup, you damn maggot!' Ganz bellowed at the drunk.

'It's a good question, Larry,' Spitter Larch said. 'Draw or back off.' He glanced at the cards he held. 'You're breaking my concentration.'

Rattled beyond good sense, Ganz snorted, 'Ain't that a real shame, Spitter.'

Ganz's rash and bone-headed rebuke of Larch, Clooney reckoned, solved his problem.

'For you it is, Ganz,' Larch snarled.

A stiletto flashed in Spitter Larch's hand from a spring mechanism up his sleeve. The blade's delivery was precise and deadly. In the blink of an eye the stiletto was buried in Larry Ganz's throat. He staggered back against the bar, clutching at the knife and wasting his last precious seconds of life trying to dislodge it. Ganz slid down the bar to the filthy cantina floor. A pool of blood spread out from him, exciting the million flies that constantly buzzed around the cantina.

Larch got up from the card-table and retrieved the stiletto. He reached across the bar and grabbed the towel slung over the keeper's shoulder. He wiped the blade clean on the greasy rag. Unconcerned, the Mexican continued with the chore of cleaning the glasses he had lined up on the bar, seeing no reason to have his task interrupted by a towel streaked with fresh blood.

When Larch turned round to take up Ganz's argument with Frank Clooney, the bounty hunter had left. Frank Clooney had already had the good fortune to have been able to throw in a bad hand, and he saw no point in drawing another from the deck on offer.

Now, under Spitter Larch's beady-eyed scrutiny, Clooney wondered if that steamy afternoon in the Nogales cantina was coming back to haunt him.

'Rafter, you say your name is?' Larch questioned.

Frank Clooney nodded. 'Sam Rafter.'

After further in-depth scrutiny, Larch said amiably: 'Howdy, Mr Rafter.'

'Are you goin' to join us, Mr Larch?' Ned Carver enquired eagerly.

'Don't mind if I do,' Larch replied.

Had Larch not recalled who he was? Clooney pondered. Or was he cruelly toying with him? Only time would tell.

CHAPTER SEVEN

About to roll, Larch asked the bounty hunter: 'Ever been south of the border, Rafter?'

'Who ain't, round these parts,' was Clooney's easy reply.

The bounty hunter saw no gain in denying familiarity with Mexico. Experience had taught him that an outright denial usually made the inquisitive more curious. Hanging out in the border region, it would be most unlikely for a man not to have crossed over a time or two to trade, or to experience the pleasures of the cantina women who, compared to their American counterparts, were more passionate and adventurous and a whole lot cheaper.

'Whereabouts?' was Spitter Larch's not unexpected next question.

Frank Clooney maintained his air of casual detachment. 'Here and there.'

Larch chuckled. 'Where's here and where's there, friend?'

The bounty hunter shrugged.

'Like I said, here and there,' he repeated.

Larch settled a long lazy look on Clooney. 'You know, if I was a suspicious man, I might think that you're avoiding an answer to my question.'

'Think what you want, Larch. It's a free country.'

Clooney was banking on a frosty rebuff to get him out of a difficult bind. It was a gamble. Larch might just take the dismissal unkindly. Clooney had seen how explosive his temper could be, and it did not take a lot to make him angry.

Seeing a potential conflict in which sides would have to be taken, Ned Carver acted as peacemaker.

'Hey, let's roll, huh?' he said amiably. 'You fellas've got lots of time to gab.'

'The man's got a point, Larch,' Clooney said.

'Guess so,' said Spitter Larch. 'I'll hitch my horse to the wagon and ride inside, Carver. The nag's been through a rough couple of days.'

'Sure,' Carver agreed exuberantly, relieved that the thorny to and fro discussion between Larch and Rafter was over, for the time being at any rate.

Clooney's problems were not over. His being trapped inside the wagon with Larch would give the outlaw the chance to continue his quizzing. The bounty hunter was casting about for a reason not to join Larch, and despairing of finding one, when Becca Carver again came to his rescue.

'You or Mr Larch take my seat,' she told Clooney, and explained to Carver: 'I'm feeling a tad queasy, Ned. You don't mind, do you, honey? The shade will be welcome for a spell.'

Grasping the way out Becca had handed him, Frank Clooney lost no time in occupying the seat Becca had vacated.

'You rest well, ma'am,' he said.

Just to make a point, Larch was of a mind to challenge for the seat, but being in close proximity to the Carver woman had its lure. He had not had a woman in over a week, and that was a long time, the outlaw being a man of vast appetite. In his chinwag with Carver, the no-good bastard had been as forthright as a man selling his wife could be, letting it be known that if the terms were right his conditions would be few, and his objections nil.

'You'd sell your wife?' Larch questioned Carver.

Carver had grinned slyly. 'A woman like Becca's saleable goods, Larch. And a man's got to make the most of what he's got to trade.'

'Your wife might have a mind of her own, Carver,' Larch had suggested.

'Then you change it the best way you know

how,' was Ned Carver's solution. 'For myself,' he snorted, 'I've always found that tamin' a clawin', scratchin' woman can be a real pleasurable pastime.'

Having planted the seed to grow, Ned Carver had taken his leave.

'We'll talk again later,' was his parting remark.

Spitter Larch had seen no point in telling Carver that, should he decide to take his wife, he'd not pay a solitary nickel for the pleasure. Money to a dead man was of no use anyway. Carver was a fool, and posed no problem. The man called Rafter, if that was his right name, was another matter. Rafter was playing a game. What game he had not yet cottoned on to. But of one thing he was sure, it was not his normal game. There was something about Rafter that made him uneasy. And a pinch of salt to a goldmine, he figured that Becca Carver was counting on Rafter to free her from Carver. She was clever. Her shrewdness had been evident in the slick way she had switched places with Rafter, helping him avoid his questions, he figured. And if that were true, then it meant that she, like him, figured that Sam Rafter had answers to give, and saw any further questions by him as having the potential to scupper her plans.

Spitter Larch leaned back, rolled a smoke and puffed in a leisurely fashion, spitting out the flecks of tobaccoo, a habit that had earned him the monicker of Spitter. It was, he decided, going to be one heck of a mighty interesting journey.

CHAPTER EIGHT

The morning stretched into afternoon with no one saying much, which suited Frank Clooney to a T. Larch seemed to spend most of the time asleep, but the bounty hunter reckoned that he was feigning slumber to allow him to listen to and sift any natter there might be. It was an old ruse, used a time or two by Clooney himself. Once, on a stage journey, the trick had been particularly useful in finding the man he was hunting down by the loose talk of his fellow passengers, consisting of rumour and half-truth which, when examined as a whole, pinpointed the man's whereabouts.

'All lost your tongues?' Ned Carver asked, grumpily swatting bugs.

'Takes all of a man's energy to just draw breath in this heat,' was Clooney's excuse for his silence.

'Yeah,' Carver agreed listlessly. 'Guess you're right at that, Rafter.'

'Besides, our gabbing might disturb Mr Larch's sleep,' the bounty hunter observed mischievously.

To his credit, Spitter Larch did not twitch a muscle. Shortly after, he emitted a long snore.

Becca Carver welcomed the lack of conversation too, because it gave her the chance to get her rambling thoughts into some sort of order. She had, despite all indications to the contrary, reckoned that Sam Rafter could help her and Emily get free of Ned Carver's evil clutches. She was certain that he was not as unmoved as he appeared to be by her and Emily's plight.

Ned Carver also had his plans. At first he thought Becca was loco, when she had made a case for taking Rafter in tow. However, she had quickly convinced him that there might be more gain than pain in having him along.

'San Gabriel,' Becca had said thoughtfully. 'Wasn't that where they struck gold a couple of years ago?'

Ned Carver shot upright on the wagon seat. 'Gold!'

Becca frowned, as if searching her mind to bring together hazy details.

'I recall something about a gold shipment that was heisted and never found. My late husband told me that in lawman circles it was said that the wagon had been hidden to be collected down the line when the heat eased off.'

Becca, suddenly as excited as a kid on Christmas morning, went on: 'You know, Ned, I figure that Rafter might just be one of those gold robbers.' Always the dreamer, Ned Carver was easily drawn into Becca's hokey yarn, the purpose of which was to keep Sam Rafter near at hand to help her when the time came to unshackle herself from Carver. 'I can't say for certain, you understand, but Rafter fits pretty well the description Daniel gave of the gang leader.'

'Don't know, Becca,' Carver had said doubtfully. 'Rafter's got the kinda face that looks familiar to ev'ryone, I reckon.'

Becca cleverly backed Carver's doubt.

'I guess so, Ned.' She counted to ten, and then began to pull in the bait. 'But heck, what if all that gold is still in San Gabriel and we let it slip through our fingers, Ned, honey?'

Her sigh was full of missed dreams.

Ned Carver was a tormented man.

'There's that poker-game in Red Sands,' he mumbled. 'I'm sure I could swindle those hicks out of a bundle.'

'Maybe that would be the safer bet, Ned. Let's leave Rafter to rot.' But, dewy-eyed, she added: 'Imagine, we'd never have to worry again about anything if that gold was there. But heck, it couldn't be. Could it?'

Ned Carver was positively feverish. Being a man

who was averse to work of even moderate demand, he spent his time turning cards and waiting for the big pot that would end all his worries and set him up in the life of ease he craved. When the cards were fickle, and his fortunes dire, he had no qualms about waylaying a man in a dark alley and slitting his throat for the change in his pocket. Now, at the mention of gold, he began to dream kingly dreams about perfumed nights on board a Fancy Dan Mississippi gambling-boat like the *Tennessee Belle*, a picture of which he had once seen in a newspaper.

Knowing well her husband's foibles, Becca Carver astutely played on them.

'You know, Ned,' she said, her eyes dreamy, 'San Gabriel isn't all that far out of our way. I reckon that with a little more push, we could check it out and still be on time for you to join that poker-game in Red Sands.'

Carver scratched his week-old stubble. 'You reckon?'

Becca shrugged. 'I guess.'

Converted, Ned Carver displayed the zeal of newly discovered beliefs.

'You're right, honey,' he enthused. He was dreaming again. 'Imagine, all that gold. All mine.' Conscious of the singular, he quickly amended, 'I mean, all ours, honey, of course.'

'All I want is your happiness, Ned,' Becca had said, looping an arm through his to hug him excitedly, the way a woman sharing a dream with her man would. 'If you're happy, that makes me happy, too.'

Ned Carver was much too preoccupied counting the fortune which he was certain now lay within his grasp to see the hate-filled contempt in which Becca held him. Animated, he leaned over to kiss her. Becca Carver heaved at the stale beer-breath that filled her mouth, and threatened to empty her stomach.

'We'll go to one of those fancy cities back East,' he said, his enthusiasm leaping. 'Live like those European kings and queens.'

'Sure we will, Ned,' Becca said, just as enthusiastic.

Carver said, testing Becca's response: 'You know if that gold is there, we'll prob'ly have to kill Rafter to get our hands on it.'

'Is that a problem, Ned?'

He grinned. 'It ain't for me.'

'Then we don't have a problem at all,' Becca Carver said.

Carver pulled her to him. 'I always knew that sooner or later you'd come round to my way of doing things, honey,' he said, winking slyly.

CHAPTER NINE

Becca thought bitterly: Why did you go and get yourself shot in the back, Daniel Scott. You should have known better than to turn your back to a dark alley. But I guess, having tamed and civilized Hawk Ridge, you figured that it's hellion days were over.

Setting aside her bitterness, Becca recalled fondly the trusting and kind man whose life she had shared for ten happy years, through the fraught times when Hawk Ridge went from being a raw, wide-open cesspool to what Daniel Scott had eventually made it – a family town, where a man could conduct his business in safety, and a woman could walk the streets without being accosted or insulted. That was why Daniel's murder was so horrendous and inexplicable. Everyone was sure that the marshal's killer was not home-grown, and that had been of some consolation to Becca in the dark days after Daniel's death. Because, had the killer proved to be a citizen of Hawk Ridge, it would have seemed that Daniel Scott had toiled in vain.

No one in Hawk Ridge, friend or foe, could understand why she had married a man of Ned Carver's low class.

'You've taken leave of your senses, Becca,' her best friend Sarah Bennett, who owned the town's dressmaking shop had said. 'There can't be any other explanation why you'd want to hitch your wagon to a toerag the likes of Ned Carver.'

Becca's reasoning was not uncommon in the West, where a woman with a man found it hard to survive, and a widow woman impossible.

'I'm a widow with a young child, Sarah. That leaves me three choices. Marriage to whoever will have me. Starvation. Or the life of a saloon woman.'

'You and Emily can come live with me,' said Sarah. 'I've got more rooms than I have use for.'

Sarah had not been the only one who had offered Becca shelter. But being a fiercely independent woman, she could not live easily with charity or worse, pity.

'Ned Carver has done the asking, Sarah,' Becca said, 'and I dare not refuse. Because there might not be another man willing to take me and Emily on.'

'Shoo!'

'You know I'm right,' Becca had told her friend. 'And you know too how finicky Western men are about taking another man's widow to their bed. Bluntly put, Sarah, there are women for pleasure and women for homemaking. And the Western man likes his homemaker to be known only to him.'

'I ain't married and I ain't starving neither,' Sarah Bennett had said spiritedly.

'It's not the same thing, Sarah. Being on the shelf by choice, and being used goods.'

Accepting Becca's logic, the dressmaker eventually dropped her opposition to Becca's plans, but with the stipulation: 'If Carver doesn't treat you or Emily right, you come back here.'

Becca had promised that she would, knowing that she would not. Marrying Ned Carver, gambler and layabout, would last until death did them part. All she could hope for was that somehow she could change Carver – make him a productive citizen. And for a time she thought that she had almost succeeded. But eventually she had had to accept that indeed, leopards did not change their spots. And now, with two years of being Mrs Ned Carver behind her, Becca often felt that the life of a saloon dove, which she had married Carver to avoid, had in essence been visited on her by him. He was a man of even cruder ways than she could have imagined. Vile and mean-tempered. At the risk of losing her immortal soul, Becca had many times knelt and prayed for her delivery from Carver's clutches, even if it meant being a widow woman again. And a time or two, she had come close to being the instrument of her own deliverance. There was that time she had reached for a pistol which had slipped from his drunken grasp. And Becca recalled the night she had stood over him while he slept in a drunken stupor, knife in hand, hurting from and dirtied by the way he had used her, wanting to slit open his throat. But she had balked at damning herself to hell. However, of late, with Emily developing quickly to a head-turning young woman, she had seen the looks Carver was giving her and regretted her lack of courage. Becca also feared that Carver would see Emily as tradeable goods. She had vowed that if damnation was to be the price she would have to pay for Emily's safety, then she would gladly pay it.

'Seen more hair on a bald man's head,' Carver grumbled, as long stretch after long stretch of flat, camp-unfriendly country rolled by. And when at last he pulled into a circle of boulders that offered little in the way of cover from prying eyes, should there be any, on seeing the doubtful glances of his fellow-travellers he growled:

'It's all there is. Ain't a soul round an'way. And

the horses are tuckered out,' he added to bolster his argument.

Clooney kept his powder dry. Spitter Larch was outspoken.

'You passed at least a dozen better spots,' he moaned.

Carver was straining at the leash to contest Larch's grouse, but his fear of the outcome of any disagreement with the mean-eyed honcho over-rode his ire, and self-preservation became his main concern.

'Reckon I got it wrong, Larch,' he said, amiably apologetic. 'Happens to a man sometimes.'

Spitter Larch's ugly gaze settled on Frank Clooney. 'You got an opinion, Rafter?'

The bounty hunter shrugged. 'I'm a man with-out a horse, Larch,' he drawled. 'That makes me a guest of Mr Carver and his good wife. So it ain't for me to complain, I figure.'

'Smooth-tongued critter, ain't ya,' was Larch's opinion.

Larch switched his gaze back to Ned Carver and maintained his critical visage for a spell longer, enjoying Carver's cringing, before snort-ing:

'Guess so, Carver.' He looked about the smooth ground within the circle of boulders. 'At least the ground ain't got too much stones.' He scratched his pointed chin, his eyes searching the flat country spreading out from the circle of boulders. 'I guess I won't have any problem spottin' the critters who are tailing me,' he concluded.

'Critters followin' you, you say?' Ned Carver worried. He figured that any pursuers Larch might have would not be the kind of guests a fella would invite into his parlour, because they'd likely be gents of Spitter Larch's own ilk. Or, Carver worried even more keenly, the men chasing Larch might be lawmen. And the law was the last thing he wanted to come face to face with. His past was littered with deeds that would interest any lawman, and a couple of deeds that would see him swing on a gallows.

One such murderous episode took his mind back to a dark alley in Hawk Ridge.

For once he had been flush, and had booked a room in the hotel instead of sleeping in the livery as he did if the livery owner was of a kindly frame of mind, or a doorway if he was not.

He recalled a visit from Marshal Daniel Scott.

'Carver, you say your name is?' Scott had questioned.

'That's right, Marshal,' he confirmed. 'Something I can do for you?'

Ned Carver had looked Scott in the eye without blinking, but was already cursing his stroke of bad luck, figuring that as soon as Scott left he'd have to hightail it out of Hawk Ridge and miss the poker-game he had unexpectedly come upon, seeing rich pickings to be swindled from a group of dumb hicks who would be slow to figure out that there were more than the standard four aces in a deck of cards. The poker-game was a yearly event, always played at the end of round-up, and was the exception to Scott's otherwise rigid enforcement of the town's no gambling laws, the marshal seeing gambling as one of the root causes of trouble.

Daniel Scott's keen gaze took in Carver's shabby valise and down-at-heel appearance.

'What line of business are you in, Mr Carver?'

Carver could see the wheels turning in the lawman's head, putting two and two together and rightly coming up with four as the answer.

'Whatever comes my way, Marshal.'

'Pretty vague, that,' Scott had said.

'In these hard times, a man's gotta keep body and soul together an'way he can, Marshal.'

'That's surely a fact,' Daniel Scott had agreed. 'Planning to stay in town long, Carver? That's what you said your name was, wasn't it?'

'Surely. And the most I'll be around for is a coupla days.'

'Play poker?'

'Now and then.'

'Planning on joining in the end-of-round-up game here in town?'

Ned Carver shrugged. 'Might sit in for a hand or two.'

Daniel Scott had smiled. 'Well, good luck.'

'Thanks, Marshal. I sure 'preciate your kind wishes.'

Carver recalled how he had almost wilted under Scott's parting gaze. He had kept watch on the marshal's office. And as he had expected, a short time later, his worst fears were confirmed when Daniel Scott headed for the telegraph office. He had listened at an open window to Scott dictating a wire to the law agency in the territorial capital. When he got the answer back, Marshal Daniel Scott would be calling on him again. And his next call would be the first step on the road to a hangman's noose.

It was dusk. The telegraph office would be closing. It would be the following morning before Scott got a reply. Good sense would dictate that he should shake off the dust of Hawk Ridge then and there, but there was a poker pot to consider; a pot which he saw no difficulty in getting his hands on. But there would be other pots to pocket in the three-day event, pots of which he was confident of relieving the local yokels. But to do that he would have to hang around, and remaining in Hawk Ridge with a curious lawman was a risk he did not intend taking. He had been in tight spots before and had wriggled free. He was confident that this time, too, old ways would prove best. He went to his valise, and extracted from a hidden pocket the knife he had used many times before. His plan was simple. The marshal, as marshals did, would make a late-night check of his town. He'd waylay him, and slit his throat.

Of course there was that reply to Scott's wire coming down the line, but he had a plan to deal with that too. There had been a long spell of dry weather. The clapboard telegraph office was bone dry; dry enough to burn furiously.

The fact that he had remained in town long enough to marry Scott's wife was proof positive of how wily a planner and how good an actor Ned Carver was.

'Andy Sweeney and his brothers,' Spitter Larch said, in reply to Carver's query about the men pursuing him.

It was news that made Carver shake in his boots.

'The Sweeneys,' he yelled, wide-eyed. 'Those honchos would slit their own mother's throat.'

'They surely would,' Larch concurred. 'Ben Sweeney shot his pa when he was only twelve years old.'

'You gotta ride out,' Carver said.

'Are you withdrawing your invitation, Carver.' Larch's stance changed a tad, but in that barely perceptible movement, his whole demeanour had changed from relatively benign to postively malignant. 'I might reckon that such a change of heart would be a mighty unfriendly gesture.'

Ned Carver looked in Frank Clooney's direction to gauge the degree of backing he would receive, should he need it. The shaking in his boots became more acute when he was met with the bounty hunter's bland expression.

Still, he asked: 'What do you reckon, Rafter?'

Frank Clooney was in a no-win bind. Siding with Carver would aggravate Larch. On the other hand, the last honchos he wanted to cross paths with were the Sweeneys. Because whereas Larch had to dredge his memory to put a name to him, the Sweeneys would have no such difficulty, him having had a skirmish with them only the previous month.

The Sweeneys were as murderous a bunch as ever rode the West. The men they would kill, if they could, but Becca and Emily Carver would be another matter. Them they would spare for as long as their lust lasted, and then kill them. Or worse, sell them across the border to a Mex brothel.

'The man asked you a question, Rafter,' Spitter Larch intoned, hollowly.

'Well, I figure that if you talk about trouble, you call down trouble,' he said, as if the argument was

not worth the bother of serious consideration,
and hoping to convince both Larch and Carver
that that was the case. 'So I say don't talk about it
until you see it. That's surely time enough in my
book, gents.'

Larch had taken a Bowie knife from his boot
and was toying with the wicked blade.

'That good enough for you, Carver?' he
rasped.

Ned Carver gulped. 'I guess Rafter's got a
point,' he gasped.

'Sensible fella, Mr Rafter,' Larch commented.
The outlaw's gaze was steady and searching. 'You
sure we ain't crossed paths before?'

'Don't recall that we have, Larch,' Frank
Clooney replied, with just the right measure of
detachment.

Carver was eager to get past the thorny impasse
which his questioning of Spitter Larch's continued presence had created.

'Guess we'd best bunk down, huh?' he
suggested.

'Guess so,' Larch agreed.

Frank Clooney's relief was every bit as great as
Carver's was, but his outward reaction was one of
nonchalance. However, as he worked to set up
camp, he felt the burn of Spitter Larch's eyes on
him, and knew that it could only be a matter of
time before the killer rooted from his subscon-

scious a name to put with the face.

After grub, Carver volunteered: 'I'll take the watch to midnight.'

'I figure I'd like the last watch. You OK with the mid watch?' Larch said to Clooney.

'Fine by me,' was the bounty hunter's easy reply.

'That's settled then,' Carver said, heading for the wagon and returning with a bottle of rotgut. 'To keep out the cold,' he explained.

'If them Sweeneys turn up, it'll help being drunk.' Larch chuckled.

Carver instantly uncorked the bottle and slugged liberally.

CHAPTER TEN

Frank Clooney spun round, rifle cocked, on hearing what he thought was the rustle of a bush but in fact was the swish of Becca Carver's nightgown.

'Sorry, ma'am,' he apologized, as Becca came up short. 'The night makes a man nervous.'

'I brewed some hot coffee,' she said, offering him a tin mug. 'It'll keep out the cold.' She shared the boulder on which Clooney was seated. 'And about being nervous, Mr Rafter. I think that you haven't got a nervous bone in your body.'

Frank Clooney grinned. 'Then you're a bad judge of a man, Mrs Carver.'

'I don't reckon that I am, Mr Rafter. And I think we should drop all this mister and ma'am business. My name is Becca, short for Rebecca.' Her gaze held Clooney's. 'Which I've always preferred my friends to call me.'

'Ma'am,' Clooney said, 'shouldn't you be lying with your husband?'

'I should surely, if I liked sleeping with a hog.'

'I don't know that it's right that a woman should think so poorly of her man.'

Becca Carver laughed sadly. 'She shouldn't, if her man was a *man*.'

'Ma'am,' Clooney said uncomfortably, 'mind my asking where this is going?'

'No. You've got a right.'

'Then I'd be mighty obliged if you'd tell me.'

'Simple, really. I want to get my daughter Emily out of Ned Carver's reach.'

'Seems all you have to do, if that's the case, is walk out when you reach the next town,' the bounty hunter said.

'Oh, come now, Sam. You know that Ned Carver isn't the kind of man you just walk out on.'

'Guess I can't argue against that, Becca,' he conceded.

'You've seen the way that Carver looks at Emily?'

Frank Clooney shifted uneasily. 'I've seen.'

'And you know exactly what that look means, don't you.'

'It ain't hard to know,' he admitted.

'Then you know that it's only a matter of time before the bastard I'm married to will have his way with her, and then likely trade her.'

'Seems that way,' Clooney agreed. 'But what business of mine that is, I'm not sure.'

Becca Carver looked Clooney steadily in the eye. 'I'm counting on you being the decent man I've got you figured for. And if I'm right, you're cringing every bit as much as me at the prospect of Emily becoming Carver's soiled goods.'

'It doesn't do for a man to poke his nose in, Becca,' he said.

'That's true. But sometimes a decent man hasn't got a choice. Don't you reckon, Sam?'

'Becca!'

Carver's drunken bawl interrupted their conversation, an interruption that Frank Clooney welcomed on one hand because it relieved him of the need to answer Becca's question, while at the same time brought a shudder to him at the thought of what faced Becca once Carver got her back inside the wagon.

'Becca, what're you doin' out and about in your nighshift talkin' to 'nother man?' Ned Carver roared furiously. He jumped down from the wagon and wobbled drunkenly towards them, vowing: 'I'll kill ya Rafter, if'n you've been toyin' with my woman.'

Becca intercepted Carver. 'We were only talking, Ned. Nothing more.'

'Yeah?' he growled, spittle dripping from his

chin. 'You expect me to believe that?'

'It's the truth, Ned.'

'I don't believe ya!' Carver's fist shot into Becca's midriff and she folded. Clooney was on his feet. Carver reached behind him for the sixgun tucked inside his trousers.

'Move 'nother inch and I'll cut you down,' he growled.

'It's as he says, Carver.' All eyes went to Spitter Larch coming out of the darkness. 'Rafter and your wife have just been gabbing, like she said.'

Ned Carver's crazed gaze switched between Larch and the bounty hunter.

'Mebbe you've both been nibblin',' he grumbled.

'Seems to me,' Larch said, 'that it's only a matter of time before that suspicious mind and loose mouth of yours will get you killed, Carver. Go back to bed, if you don't want that to happen right now.'

Frank Clooney saw the flash of temptation light in Becca Carver's eyes. He shook his head. But by so doing, knew that by staying her hand now, he had in the longer term committed himself to helping her.

'Git!' Carver hauled Becca to her feet and shoved her ahead of him to the wagon.

'Obliged, Larch,' Clooney said. 'You probably saved my life.'

'Don't thank me,' the outlaw said. 'I'm only keeping you round until I can put a name to that dial of yours, mister. Then I guess I might have to kill you myself.'

CHAPTER ELEVEN

'Riders coming!' Emily Carver's warning rang alarm bells. Her holler brought a hurried end to breakfast, and a quick dash to arms. 'Three.'

Ned Carver paled.

'How many Sweeney brothers is there?' he quizzed Larch.

'Four,' Becca Carver said. And when general amazement was expressed that she, a mere woman, should be the possessor of such information, she explained: 'I was a marshal's wife. Desperadoes and their shenanigans was often table talk when a fellow lawman visited with Daniel.'

Carver relaxed. 'Can't be the Sweeneys, then.'

His relief was quickly shattered by Spitter Larch's startling update.

'Used to be four, before I killed Ike Sweeney, the youngest of the bunch.'

Carver staggered back against the wagon.

'There's a spare rifle in the wagon,' Becca told Clooney, and went to fetch it.

Taking the rifle and picking a spot, Frank Clooney was beginning to think that fate had dealt him a lousy hand, which might just be the last one in the deck of life.

'If we're fast and accurate, we can cut them down before they get too close,' was Ned Carver's strategy.

'And what if they're innocent travellers, Ned?' Becca asked.

'It'll be their tough luck, won't it,' he growled.

'It will be cold-blooded murder,' Becca retorted spiritedly. 'That's what it will be.'

'Do you want to wait around until you're looking the Sweeneys in the eye, woman?' Carver fumed. 'I know that I damn well don't.' Seeking backing for his cowardly plan, he asked: 'Do you fellas?'

'Ma'am, your husband's right,' Spitter Larch said.

'Hah!' Carver scoffed triumphantly.

'It's been my long experience that waiting usually ends in suffering,' Larch continued.

Now it was Becca's turn to seek support for her stand.

'Mr Rafter, I'd like to hear what you have to say?'

'He don't count none,' Ned Carver snorted.

'Not for much, sure enough,' was Larch's sneering opinion. 'But a man's got a right to his say-so, I reckon.'

Frank Clooney was of a mind to tell the notorious killer that, were he of such a democratic frame of mind now, his conversion had to have been very recent.

'Sam,' Becca urged.

Frank Clooney knew that his answer, the only one his conscience would allow him give, was destined to raise eyebrows and get Carver and particularly Larch thinking all the more.

'I figure that, as Becca says, cutting the riders down before they have a chance to be positively identified as trouble, would indeed be cold-blooded murder.'

Becca Carver shook her head in agreement, and with pride. Her assessment of Sam Rafter, as she knew him to be, had been right. The warm glow in her gaze when she looked at him pleased Clooney more than any pleasure had done in a long time. And the equally admiring glow in Emily Carver's eyes was a bonus that added greatly to his pleasure. But there was a counter balance to his pleasure. Letting the Sweeneys, if that's who the fast approaching riders were, ride in, meant that his cover would be blown sky high. And though his only motivation up to now was to reach San Gabriel in the hope of finding a nag and his way home, what he now feared most of all was Becca and Emily Carver finding out that he was a bounty hunter. He was certain that such a man, in their eyes, would make him a man to be despised.

In the social order of the West, bounty hunters had a very low standing; as low in reality as the men they hunted down. And though he had always given the men he had hunted down the chance to surrender, most had chosen to fight it out, prefer-ring to stand and fight where he had cornered them, than face the ignominy of a gallows. And he reckoned that it would do no good at all him telling Becca that the hunting down of his first man had enabled him to hold on to a patch of Arizona dirt that he had hoped he could turn to productive soil. When the farm failed and was repossessed, there wasn't much more that he could do to keep body and soul together but hunt down another man or starve. However, over the years, he had taken what little pride his work would allow him to take, from the fact that he bounty hunted only out of neccessity, and the fact that the men he hunted were men who had forfeited all right to join the ranks of civilized folk.

'Like I said, woman,' Carver raged, 'Rafter's opinion don't count for nothin' an'way. Ain't that so, Larch?'

Larch did not answer Carver's question, because his scrutiny of Clooney was burningly intense.

'Oh, to hell with all of ya!'

Ned Carver dived behind a boulder and opened fire before anyone could stop him. The report of Carver's gunfire spurred Larch to join him. Carver's shooting had been wild and inaccurate, but that was not the case with Spitter Larch's lead. Though his shot was every inch as quick as Carver's had been, his aim bore no resemblance. The middle rider of the three clutched at his chest and toppled from his saddle, as did the other riders on Larch's second and third shots. Three shots. Three dead. As a shooter, Spitter Larch's skill had to be admired. But as a man he had to be despised. The oncoming riders had had no chance at all.

'I'll be damned,' Carver exclaimed, prancing around joyfully. He back-slapped Larch. 'That was some fancy shootin', friend. Remind me to never get in your darn gunsights.'

'Your rejoicing might be premature, Carver,' said Clooney.

'What d'ya mean?' he asked sharply.

'That first rider that Larch downed was no more than a boy.'

'So?' Carver grunted.

'What Rafter is trying to tell you, Carver, is that

the boy wore a head band, ain't that so?' Larch said.

'That's so,' Frank Clooney confirmed.

'So?' Carver repeated aggressively. Then his annoyance turned to worry. 'Bareback horse,' he repeated slowly. 'Headband . . .' Then he swallowed hard. 'Shit. An Indian boy?'

'An Apache boy,' Larch said.

'What was an 'pache doin' ridin' with the Sweeneys?' Carver questioned, his panic shooting up.

'They weren't the Sweeneys.'

'Yeah?' Spitter Larch intoned. 'Now how come you know that, Rafter?'

Frank Clooney cursed his careless mouth. His admission had started Larch thinking all the more.

'Saw the Sweeneys in Tombstone,' he lied.

'Tombstone, huh?' Larch pondered. 'They never mentioned no trip to Tombstone to me.'

'Then I guess they didn't tell you everything,' Clooney said with a casual drawl.

'Guess not,' Larch said. 'Can you recall when the Sweeneys made this trip to Tombsto—'

'Does it matter?' Becca Carver cut in sharply. 'We've got trouble on our doorstep, and this is no time for small talk.'

'Becca's darn well right,' Ned Carver growled. 'You fellas can work out when the damn Sweeneys were in Tombstone 'nother time. It's of no darn importance now.'

Spitter Larch fixed Frank Clooney with a stare. 'I ain't none too sure 'bout that, Carver,' he said meaningfully.

Ned Carver, a shrewd *hombre*, was quick to catch Larch's drift. His gaze settled on Frank Clooney, black peeble eyes boring into him.

'Let's break camp and make tracks,' was Becca's suggestion, her worried glance going Emily's way. 'The sooner we put distance between us and those dead men, the better it will be.'

'Your woman's making sense, Carver,' Larch said. 'But first I figure I saw one of them critters move a second ago.' He slid the .45 he was packing from its holster. 'Best be sure than sorry, I say.' He began to walk towards the fallen trio.

'You're going to shoot a wounded man?' The contemptuous question had been spat out by Emily Carver.

'Close your eyes and block your ears if it bothers you that much, girl,' Larch barked. 'But I ain't taking no chance on that honcho sucking air long enough to tell the Indians the trail we took.'

'Makes sound sense,' Ned Carver agreed.

'It's murder plain and simple,' was Emily Carver's verdict.

'Emily's got a point, Ned,' Becca said.

'Yeah,' he growled sourly. 'You want 'paches

catchin' up with you and the brat?' Becca shivered and hugged herself. 'Figured not.' Carver snorted triumphantly. 'You go kill that bastard, Mr Larch. I'll hitch up the team and be ready to roll when you've taken care of matters.'

'You're wasting time,' Clooney opined. Larch and Carver spun round to face him. He looked to the sun shooting into the sky. 'Even if he is alive, how long do you figure he'll remain so in this god-forsaken hellhole?'

He looked into the empty spaces of the desert country.

'There could be Indians watching us right now. Or a dozen other equally deadly critters, alerted by your gunfire.'

Ned Carver pivoted about in a complete circle, his fright-bulged eyes sweeping the empty and desolate terrain.

'Don't see no one,' he said, a brittle crack in his voice.

'You won't see Indians until they want you to see them,' Clooney said. 'And if they're Apaches, you won't see them until they're at your shoulder to take your scalp, Carver.'

'Shit!' he swore. 'Forget that man,' he told Larch. 'Let's roll right now.'

'Are you willing to take the chance on him being dead by the time Indians find him?' Spitter Larch argued with Carver.

'I'll take my chances,' was Carver's terrified retort. 'Like Rafter said, he'll prob'ly be long dead by the time he's found.' Larch was about to press his argument but Carver, driven now by raw fear, spat, 'If'n you want Larch, take your nag and go your own way.'

Not used to sass from weasles like Ned Carver, Larch's anger flared briefly. Under different circumstances he might have killed Carver then and there, but the reason he did not was in his words. 'Sticking together makes more sense, until this dangerous impasse is over with.'

As they prepared to break camp, Becca Carver surprised Clooney in a brief moment side by side by asking:

'Who are you really?'

'Sam Rafter,' Clooney said.

Becca Carver considered the bounty hunter.

'I think that Sam Rafter is not your real name,' she stated.

Clooney had a short-lived urge to come clean and tell Becca who and what he was, but he quickly smothered the impulse. The hours and days ahead might be fraught with danger; the kind of danger that could make a secret a trade-able commodity. There was no way that the twists and turns in events could be calculated with any degree of certainty. The same need as had moti-vated his deception to begin with had not changed – in fact that need had become even more acute. Were circumstances to work out in such a way that Becca would be forced or chose to break a confidence, he could find himself stranded without a horse or a gun, and as good as dead.

'Ain't no mystery about me, Becca,' Clooney lied.

'I don't care who you are or what you've done,' she said. 'All I'm hoping for is that when the time comes, which it surely will, you'll help me and Emily to escape Ned Carver's clutches.' Her blue eyes filled with apprehension. 'And I figure the way he's been looking at Emily, Larch's clutches too.'

'Climb on board, Becca,' Ned Carver hollered. 'Now!'

'Will you help me and Emily?' Becca asked Clooney sincerely.

'Maybe,' he said in a sombre tone.

'Maybe?'

'I haven't made up my mind yet, Becca.'

'Please, Sam. I've got no other name for you. I'm begging for your help.'

Becca Carver's eyes filled up. She turned and hurried away to join Carver on the wagon.

CHAPTER TWELVE

Frank Clooney regretted his bluntness, but being a man loath to promise if there was any chance of not delivering on that promise, he reckoned that it would have been unfair to hike Becca Carver's expectations of release from her cruel husband's clutches. Besides, even if he had agreed to help her, he might not be in a position to do so when the time came to act. Carver, a lowdown bully, would not be difficult to chastise, but he had no doubt about how difficult a task it would be to overcome Spitter Larch's opposition, should that *hombre* decide to throw in his lot with Carver when he played his hand. Whereas Carver would, Clooney reckoned, turn tail when the going got rough enough, Larch, being a born killer and troubler-seeker, would revel in the chance to spill blood – any man's blood. It didn't matter whose.

Just when, as previously, Clooney was about to

have Larch as a travelling partner in the back of the wagon, Becca Carver swooned as if overcome with the heat and requested that Carver should let her ride inside the wagon.

'You ain't got nothin' in your belly, have ya?' Carver asked crudely.

Becca blushed to the roots of her hair.

'Shush, Ned,' she pleaded. 'We've got company along.'

Ned Carver's sneering countenance left no doubt of what he thought about the company of which Becca spoke.

'You been gettin' a lot of them poorly spells of late, woman. You sure?'

'Yes, Ned,' Becca snapped. 'I'm sure.'

'See,' he growled, latching on to Becca's snappish retort, 'you've been real tetchy, too. Sure sign of a woman carryin'. And if that's what's wrong with ya, then do somethin'. One brat in tow is enough to have to put up with.'

'Seems to me that a man should be proud that his seed might have found favour in a woman like Mrs Carver.'

Ned Carver glared at Frank Clooney. 'That a fact, Rafter?' he snarled.

'In my book it is,' the bounty hunter declared.

'Thank you, Mr Rafter,' Becca said, her blushes even greater than when Carver had made his crude remarks a moment earlier.

'My pleasure, Becca,' Clooney said, touching his hat.

Emily Carver smiled warmly at him, obviously thinking that the compliment might have more substance than a mere social nicety. And Frank Clooney wondered if Emily Carver might be right? He had noticed that he had become ever more ready to spring to Becca Carver's defence, the way a man smitten would.

Carver's suspicious glance flicked back and forth between Clooney and his wife with the speed of a rattler's fangs, unsure of what meaning he should take from Clooney's support for Becca. Larch, lazy-eyed, sat waiting to see if the powder-keg which Rafter's actions had uncapped would explode or prove to be a damp squib.

Damp squib was the result.

'You're a real smooth-tongued fella, Rafter, ain't ya,' Carver said with a chuckle that had about as much mirth in it as a grain of desert sand has water. 'Bet the ladies just love you.'

'I've had my moments,' Clooney drawled.

Carver's chuckle died. 'The thing about a man havin' his moments, Rafter, is that he's got to be real careful about who them moments are spent with.' He unfurled the whip he was holding, and its crack reverberated in the still, hot air. 'Let's turn wheels!'

Larch joined Carver on the wagon seat.

'I'm tempted to dump you right here in the desert, Rafter,' Ned Carver growled. 'But I figure that later I might want to kill you.'

'You know, Carver,' Frank Clooney said wearily, 'you're going to be at the end of a long queue, my friend.'

'I ain't your friend!'

'You surely called that right,' the bounty hunter snorted.

It was later that afternoon when Emily Carver saw the smoke rising from the hills to the south.

' 'Pache smoke?' Carver's question was addressed to Spitter Larch.

Larch nodded. 'I guess.'

'What's it sayin'?' was Ned Carver's next concern.

Larch made a big deal of studying the smoke, before he said, 'Ain't nothin' much. Just 'paches gabbing like old women.'

'They ain't sayin' nothin' 'bout the 'pache boy we killed?'

'No, Carver,' Larch said. 'Just gab.'

Ned Carver began to breathe easy. He wiped the treacle-thick perspiration from his face. 'Ah! I guess we'll be long gone 'fore they find that Indian boy, don't you think?'

The question was thrown out for anyone to come back with a comforting answer.

'Prob'ly be suppin' with the devil before that happens,' Larch said.

'Yeah,' Carver sighed. 'We'd best be lookin' for a place to spend the night.'

'There's a dry creek about two miles from here. I figure we should head for it,' Spitter Larch opined.

'Sounds good to me,' Carver enthusiastically agreed.

'There's more smoke now,' Emily declared, pointing due west and nearer to where they were.

Ned Carver's return to a state of anxiety was immediate, but Larch again lied with the ease of long experience.

'I told you, Carver. Just 'pache gab.'

'You sure 'bout that?' Carver fretted.

'I've been reading Indian smoke for as long as I can remember,' was Spitter Larch's reassuring guarantee; a guarantee that was as false as a wooden leg.

'Let's head for that creek, then,' Carver said, readily accepting the killer's reassurance.

Frank Clooney wondered why Larch had lied. He too could read smoke, and the messages rising off the hills were a lot more than Apache gab, as Larch had claimed. The boy who had been killed had been found, and his identity was being flashed into the desert sky. The boy was the son of a scalp-hunting bastard by the name of

Bold Eagle – the Apache renegade who had rejected all talk of a truce with the white man, preaching that all white eyes had to be driven from Indian lands or be buried in them.

'Is Larch telling the truth, Sam?' Clooney looked deep into Becca Carver's troubled eyes. 'And don't you go spinning me a yarn about not reading the smoke,' she warned. 'I saw the way you looked at Larch when he told Ned what he wanted to hear. It's not just gab, is it?'

'No,' Clooney admitted.

'They've found the Apache boy, haven't they?'

The bounty hunter nodded.

Becca Carver's eyes flashed Emily Carver's way. 'How bad is it really, Sam?'

'The dead boy is the son of an Apache called Bold Eagle.' The blood drained from Becca Carver's face, leaving in its wake a greyness that counted her years off in the blink of an eye. 'I can see that you know who he is, Becca. But this is wide-open country. Finding us will be akin to finding that needle in a haystack, I reckon.'

'Don't try and fool me, Sam,' Becca said, annoyed. 'I'm no fool. Apache trackers are the best there are, and they're looking for us right now.' She clutched at Clooney's arm. 'Promise me one thing, Sam,' she begged. 'If you can, for pity's sake, don't let them take Emily.'

'I promise, Becca,' he said.

And knowing the awful horror that white women suffered at the hands of the Apache, it was a promise he had no hesitation in giving or keeping. And if it looked like he'd have to act on his promise about Emily, it would also mean that he'd save a second bullet for Becca Carver.

CHAPTER THIRTEEN

The journey to the creek which Larch had mentioned, was an edgy trek.

'There's a canyon we can cut through to shorten the journey,' Larch advised Carver.

'A canyon, huh?' Carver fretted, his mind filled with hair-raising tales of Indian massacres in canyons. Only a year previously, shortly before the truce with the Apache was signed, there was the loss of over a hundred troopers whose captain had had the bright idea of shortening the miles back to the fort through a canyon. He had images of rocks full of lurking Indians that loosened his bowels. 'I don't reckon that that's such a good idea,' he told Larch.

'Better than open country where we can be seen for miles.'

'If the Indians are only gabbing, as you claim,' Becca said, 'what's the problem, Mr Larch?'

'Yeah,' Carver said, suspiciously.

Larch settled furious eyes on Becca Carver, and then switched his gaze to Frank Clooney. He had seen Becca in worried conversation with the bounty hunter, and it was not difficult for him to guess the content of their talk.

'OK. They found the boy,' he admitted.

Ned Carver's face drained of blood. 'You said—'

'I lied. Didn't want to make your nerves raw. I was right,' he told Carver. 'Look how damn jittery you are.'

Falteringly, Carver asked, 'W-who i-is this b-boy?'

'Bold Eagle's son,' Larch said, not sparing Ned Carver's nerves. 'A scalp-hunter if ever there was one.'

Carver seemed to shrink inside himself.

'We're all dead,' he whined.

'If we stay in open country we are,' was Spitter Larch's opinion.

'What do you say, Sam?' Becca asked Clooney.

The bounty hunter was very conscious of his earlier decision to cut short his journey by heading through a canyon; a decision that had pitched him right into the mess he now found himself in. But on this occasion, his view concurred with Larch's.

'The canyon might be a good or a bad choice,' he opined. 'But, as Larch said, open country is probably the worst choice of all.'

'And if that canyon is full of scalp-hunting 'paches?' was Carver's concern. 'What the heck then, huh?'

'Riding this country is a risky business at the best of times, Carver,' Larch said lazily. He looked at Clooney. 'Ain't that so, Rafter?'

The bounty hunter did not waste his breath putting on a show of innocence. Spitter Larch was a shrewd *hombre*. To have survived for as long as he had in his line of work was evidence of that.

'I guess that states it, sure enough, folks,' Clooney said.

'More smoke.' Larch was looking to the hills behind them.

'What's it sayin'?' Carver pleaded.

Larch said, 'Maybe Rafter will tell us.'

'Rafter?'

'Sure, Carver,' Larch said. 'Rafter can read smoke real good. Ain't that so?' he put to Clooney.

The bounty hunter looked to the smoke puffing off the hills; at a guess, only about ten miles behind them, which was no distance at all to a fast riding Indian with an intimate knowledge of the terrain.

'What're they saying, Sam?' Becca questioned urgently.

'That they've spotted us, Becca.'

'Oh, God,' Becca moaned.

'Shuddup, woman!'

Carver raised his arm to strike Becca. Clooney grabbed his arm and yanked it back.

'There's no call for that,' he rebuked Carver.

Massaging his injured arm, Ned Carver said spitefully:

'I knowed it. You and my wife's got a fire goin' for each other.'

Becca Carver did not bother to deny her husband's charge. And when she looked at Frank Clooney, his denial caught in his throat. Carver grabbed a rifle from the wagon and pointed it squarely at the bounty hunter.

'I'm unarmed,' Clooney reminded him.

'That's the way I like it to be,' Carver sneered.

'You'd kill an unarmed man?' Clooney asked, knowing the answer.

'I ain't never lost no sleep 'bout it,' Carver sniggered. He turned to Becca. 'Not even on that night I slit your husband's throat, honey.'

Becca Carver was rocked by the shock of Carver's cruel revelation.

'Had no choice, you see,' Carver explained. 'Scott came to my hotel room, real suspicious he was, too. Then I saw him go to the telegraph office to send a wire. I figured that when the answer came back, he'd sling me in jail, or worse.'

He feigned innocence.

'You see, honey, I ain't exactly been an upstanding citizen of this here United States. So I had to kill your man.'

He laughed evilly.

'It was real easy. Him standin' at the mouth of that alley, his back to me. I just snuck up, I'm good at that. Silent as a ghost, I was.'

Emily's clawing leap on to Ned Carver's back gave Clooney the chance to pounce on him. He delivered a jaw-shattering fist, the force of which catapulted Carver on to the flat of his back on the hard ground. Enraged by his willingness to cut him down in cold blood, Clooney dragged Carver to his feet and laid into him, delivering blow after crunching blow.

'Step aside, Sam!'

Becca Carver's no-quarter-given command cracked with the ferocity of a bullwhip. He turned to face Becca, standing behind him holding a cocked rifle.

'If you shoot him down like the dog he is,' Clooney counselled Becca, 'you'll be no better than he is.'

'He deserves no mercy!'

'That's true,' Clooney conceded, 'but what's to be gained by becoming like him, Becca?'

He reached out to take the rifle, but Becca pulled back, undecided, her desire to avenge Daniel Scott's murder clashing with knowing how wrong her action would be.

'Mr Rafter is right,' Emily Carver said. 'Kill him, and you'll be no better. That's not what Pa would want.'

Weeping bitterly, Becca dropped the rifle and clutched Emily to her. They wept together.

The distraction had given Ned Carver time to gather his wits, and he made good use of the opportunity, sliding from his pocket a derrigner which had got him out of many a tight spot at the gambling-tables, when some quick-witted gent who could count beyond four discovered that there were more aces in the deck than there should be.

'Drop it, Carver!'

Frank Clooney spun round. Carver was itching to use the derringer.

'I said drop it,' Larch ordered again, holding a cocked .45 on Carver.

Ned Carver dropped the gun. 'That's sure a surprise,' he told Larch, 'you sidin' with Rafter.'

Larch declared, 'I ain't siding with no one. I figure that we're going to need all the fire power we can muster, that's all.'

As mad as a bee trapped inside a bottle, Clooney charged Carver to resume his chastisement of him.

'Rein in, Rafter!' Spitter Larch commanded. The bounty hunter stopped in his tracks, glowering at Larch, helpless under the threat of his pistol. 'You'll get your chance to settle scores. Unless, of course, I kill you first. Can't say for sure why I'd want to do that. But something inside this head of mine says that there's a reason. Just don't know what it is yet.'

'Give me a gun and we'll settle it right now, Larch,' Clooney rasped.

'That's a mighty tempting offer, Rafter. But like I said, we're going to need all the shooting-irons we've got.' After a moment's consideration, he added: 'Tell you what, if we keep our scalps we'll settle scores.' He chuckled. 'Even if I don't know what score there is to settle.'

Carver stood sullen, no doubt plotting evil. The smoke from the hills was getting thicker as messages flashed between renegade Apaches.

'Let's head for that canyon fast,' was Larch's advice; advice that Clooney contradicted.

'That canyon will be crawling with Indians.'

'And how do you know that?' Larch growled, obviously not used to having his orders questioned.

'The top of that canyon is the only high point around here, and Indians need height to send their smoke,' the bounty hunter reasoned.

'You damn dumbhead!' Carver roared at Larch.

Reacting, Larch said: 'That makes two I'll have

114

to kill, if we get out of this bind we're in.'

Carver displayed the bravado of a man beyond caring.

'We can settle it right now, Larch!' he said.

Spitter Larch snorted. 'You must want to die real bad, mister.'

'Better to die right now than be roasted slowly over an Apache fire.' The voicing of the graphic scenario shocked Becca, and she drew a frightened Emily into her arms. Bitter as crucifixion gall, Carver did not spare them. 'Of course, every damn Indian will have you both a hundred times before they roast you.' He sneered at Becca and maliciously added: 'The young ones they really like.'

'You know, Carver,' Frank Clooney barked, 'I've known a lot of men who deserved to die, but none more so than you.'

Carver pulled a knife from his boot and slung it at the bounty hunter. Clooney ducked, but he felt the breeze of the blade brush his left cheek. The knife thudded into the side of the wagon. Its blade snapped, so venomous had Carver's throw been. Clooney dived for Carver, and might very well have acted on his statement about him deserving to die, had not Larch's call taken precedence.

'Indians!'

On a rise of ground with ambitions to be a hill,

south of where they were, two Apaches were watching them.

'Scouts,' Larch said.

Carver grabbed a rifle.

'Don't waste your lead,' Clooney said. 'They'll have vanished long before your bullet gets anywhere near them. Besides, at this distance, your chances of hitting your target with any fatal results are zero.'

'They're scouts,' Carver screamed, as near to outright hysteria as didn't matter. 'Indians will be swarmin' all over us in no time at all.'

'The sound of gunfire will have the same effect,' Clooney said. 'All we can hope for is that the main raiding party is not too close at hand. Meanwhile, we'd better head for that creek, pronto.'

Larch played the devil's advocate.

'We could be rolling right into trouble, Rafter.'

'Whatever we do now might be the wrong option,' the bounty hunter replied. 'But one thing's for sure. If we hang around here, it will be the worst option of all.'

Clooney climbed on board the wagon, and grabbed the reins.

'And what the hell d'ya think you're doin'?' Carver challenged him.

'You're as jittery as a man with a rattler in his trousers, Carver,' Clooney said in a no-nonsense tone. 'You'd run this rig into trouble. Hunker down inside.'

Spitter Larch, who seemed to be enjoying the mounting crisis with the degree of relish that only a man with a strong streak of loco in him could, chuckled.

'Mule-willed fella, ain't you, Rafter,' he commented. 'I figure that the man you've been hiding all along is now coming to the fore.' He let out a long sigh. 'The thing is, why would you want us good folk to think that you were something you ain't?'

Carver laughed insanely. 'I'll tell you why, Larch. It's 'cause of all that gold.'

Larch tensed. 'Gold?'

'Yeah. Lotsa gold. A whole damn wagon of gold.'

'A wagon, huh? That sure is a lot of gold, Carver.' He studied Frank Clooney. 'Interesting yarn, ain't it.'

'Tell him, Becca,' Carver urged. All eyes were on Becca Carver. 'Well, what're you waitin' for? Tell Larch, like you told me.'

'What I told you was all hokey, Ned,' Becca confessed. 'There isn't any wagon of gold in San Gabriel.'

Carver, stunned, mumbled, 'But you said that that lawman husband of yours—'

'There's no gold, Ned,' Becca restated emphatically.

117

'Then why. . . ?' Carver's loco eyes flashed to Frank Clooney. 'You just wanted him along, didn't you?'

'Yes, Ned,' Becca admitted.

'Whore!'

'It's not like that,' Becca said. 'The fact is that I was counting on Sam Rafter to get me and Emily away from your evil clutches.'

'And how did you aim to do that?' Carver asked, mean-mouthed.

'God help me, Ned. I didn't care how.'

Frank Clooney now had the explanation for Ned Carver's change of mind, and that explanation told him how resourceful a woman Becca Carver was. He preferred *resourceful* to cunning. And he preferred *desperate* to ruthless. Because he was beginning to nurture the hope that Becca might be part of his future. It had not been decided yet, and would not be until he was sure that there was a future for him or anyone else.

On hearing Becca Carver's cold-blooded admission, Spitter Larch's admiration for her took a leap. Possessing such a fine-looking woman, he had thought a bonus. However, such grit and cunning, added to her other womanly attributes, made her a prize worth risking death for. He had counted on having the snivelling cur Carver to deal with when he made his move on Becca, and he posed little difficulty. Now, however, having heard the admiration for Rafter in Becca's voice, and having seen Rafter's warm look at her, he figured that to make Becca Carver his woman he would have to fight Sam Rafter for her. So be it. But Rafter was a much tougher proposition than Carver. His holster was empty. Carver had somehow relieved him of his gun, but he wore his gunbelt like a second skin, the way a gun-handy man did. And the polished leather of the holster was indicative of his having drawn that gun often. Now if he was gun-handy, had drawn a gun often, and was still sucking air . . .

Well, that made Sam Rafter, a very dangerous man indeed.

'All aboard,' Clooney ordered.

Larch unhitched his horse and mounted up. 'It'll be less weight for the team to pull,' he said.

But Clooney wondered whether that was the real reason for Larch's change of transport. Under the present threat of danger a fresh horse would be an asset worth more than gold, so it made no sense to tire him, even a little. Boarding his horse had given Spitter Larch independence of movement. Perhaps, if an Indian attack came, he planned on bolting? Or maybe he had other plans, like grabbing Becca Carver and bolting. He had always reckoned that at some point, Larch would want to satisfy his lust, and when his urge got strong enough Ned Carver would not stand in his way.

Larch was no fool, and even if he were the idiot of all idiots, he could not have missed the meaning in Becca Carver's eyes when she had looked at him, and that meant that if Larch wanted Becca he would have to deal with him. On the wagon seat, he would be a slow moving, sitting target. Larch, mounted, would have greater mobility and be a fast moving target. Harder to hit. His move from wagon to saddle had given the outlaw a distinct advantage.

'I'll ride inside with Ned,' Becca said, moved by pity on seeing her husband's pitiful slide into apathy.

'Is it OK if I ride with you, Mr Rafter?' Emily asked.

'I guess, Emily. But you do as I say if there's a sign of trouble, you hear?'

'Surely will, Mr Rafter.'

They had been rolling along for about ten minutes when Emily whispered:

'Are you in love with my ma, Mr Rafter?'

CHAPTER FOURTEEN

Frank Clooney gulped. He glanced back into the wagon, but it seemed that Becca had not heard her daughter's question.

'What kind of question is that for a nipper to ask?' he scolded Emily.

'A sensible one,' she said. 'Seeing that if you love my ma, that will make you my pa.'

'You've already got a pa.'

'Ned Carver isn't my pa,' Emily declared in a vehement whisper. 'Never was and never will be!' Her blazing eyes glared at Clooney. 'And I'm none too sure what kind of a pa you'll make either. But you've got to be better than him.'

Emily Carver's eyes rolled to indicate the inside of the wagon. Clooney glanced back. Becca was talking softly to Ned Carver, but her words were making no impression on her vacant-eyed husband. Stark guilt was etched on Becca's face.

'Don't know why Ma is so bothered,' Emily said. 'You don't nurse a rabid dog.'

'She's bothered, young woman,' Clooney berated Emily, 'because she's a damn fine and good woman.'

Emily's smile was broad and knowing.

'You do love my ma,' she crooned smugly.

Spitter Larch drew alongside.

'Dust,' he said.

Clooney craned his head round the side of the wagon to where Larch had pointed. A plume of fast-moving dust floated on the dead desert air. 'I reckon about a half hour's ride to catch us up.'

'How far is this creek you've been talking about?'

'Five, maybe six miles.'

The bounty hunter looked to the deep wagon-wheel tracks in the sandy terrain.

'This wagon isn't moving fast enough to make it,' was his view.

'Unladen, maybe,' Larch opined.

Clooney shook his head. 'Even unladen.'

'That leaves the canyon,' Larch said.

Clooney looked again at the dust cloud. 'How many do you figure?'

Larch shrugged.

'Manageable, maybe?' Clooney considered.

'I can shoot,' Emily volunteered eagerly, her blue eyes dancing.

Condescendingly, Frank Clooney ruffled her dark hair.

'Don't rub my head like a kid,' she rebuked him, and insisted: 'I can damn well shoot, and shoot straight too. He showed me how.' Her head nodded in the direction of Carver. 'Said that when he was drunk, which was most of the time, I'd have to protect Ma.' Her face curled in distaste. 'Should've shot him first.'

'Hush, Emily,' Becca scolded her daughter. 'I'll have none of that talk, you hear?'

'You're not going soft on him, are you, Ma?' Emily asked in disgust.

'Ned's not right in the head, can't you see that?'

'Sure I can see that,' Emily replied argumentatively. 'But he never was right in the head to start with.'

'You're ma's right, Emily,' Clooney said. 'Talk like you've been talking isn't becoming the young lady your ma reared.'

Spitter Larch intervened impatiently.

'I suggest that you folk argue later,' he rasped.

'He's right,' Clooney said. 'Let's make tracks for the canyon, and hope that those Apaches have more ground to cover than it looks like.' He frowned worriedly. 'And that when we get there we won't ride into a nest of the bloodthirsty varmints!'

The bounty hunter laid a whip on the team, feeling pity for the tired horses, but under the circumstances unable to afford respite. The wagon's roll was spritely enough at the beginning, but it soon became sluggish as the team's energy flagged.

'Use more whip,' was Larch's solution, now scanning the country to the rear every couple of seconds.

'Do that and the horses will collapse.'

'That dust cloud is getting closer by the second.' There was a keen edge of anxiety to the normally unflappable outlaw. 'Unless those nags pick up the pace, we're not going to make it to the canyon,' he warned direly.

Frank Clooney had long ago expected Spitter Larch to take off. It certainly wasn't chivalry that was keeping him around. He'd have left his own mother at the mercy of the Apaches if it meant saving his own hide. So that left only one explanation for his lingering – Becca Carver. With time ticking away, and his chances of escaping the Indians getting fewer with every passing second, it could only be a short time now before Larch made his move.

'I feel a wobble on the rear left wheel,' Clooney said. The outlaw swallowed hard, and his eyes became shifty. 'Check it out will you, Larch?'

Larch swung the mare and headed back along.

Clooney leaned into the wagon, grabbed a rifle and put it under the seat.

Becca Carver's sharp intake of breath got the bounty hunter's attention. And when he saw what she was holding he gulped, mesmerized by the ugly trophy. It was the black and bloated severed finger of the woman George Watkins had raped and murdered. The grim evidence of George Watkins's demise had fallen out of his waistcoat pocket when he had leaned into the wagon. Becca's look of horror and contempt cut deep into Clooney.

'My name isn't Rafter,' he hurriedly explained. 'My real name is Clooney – Frank Clooney.'

'The bounty hunter?'

Clooney nodded.

'Daniel used to talk about you. Used to say that you were the best in the business.' Her face curled, as if she had eaten something nasty. 'But I wouldn't take that as a reference, Mr Clooney.'

Disgusted, she dropped the severed finger.

'The law requires proof, Becca,' he said. 'This is hot country. Watkins, the man who cut that finger off, would have rotted in no time. And having him in tow would bring every scavenger for miles around.'

'All this time you lied,' Becca said.

'I had no choice. I was horseless in desert country. Would you have had me along if you knew

125

who I really was? Would you?' he pressed, when Becca did not answer his question.

'No,' she admitted at last.

Larch was coming back.

'Don't say a word,' he implored. 'We'll talk later.'

'You're even worse than Ned Carver!' was Emily's verdict.

Larch was sour and suspicious. 'There ain't nothing wrong with that wheel, Rafter.'

'His name isn't Rafter, Mr Larch,' Becca said.

'Oh, yeah. What is it then?'

'Frank Clooney.'

Spitter Larch stiffened. He had heard many tales of Clooney's persistence and proficiency.

'Mr Clooney is a—'

'I know what he is,' Larch spat. 'A low-down bounty hunter.'

Emily held up the severed finger. 'He had this in his pocket.'

Larch took the grisly item, undisturbed by its gruesomeness, but excited by the sparkling diamond adorning it. To Becca and Emily Carver's amazement, Larch pocketed the finger.

'A good diamond always fetches a nice penny.' He addressed Clooney.

'You must have killed George Watkins to get this.' He sniggered. 'Heard all about him being kind of rushed after raping that schoolmarm.' A sixgun flashed in Larch's right hand. 'Draw rein,' he ordered, 'and unhitch the horses.'

Becca Carver, in deep shock, asked, 'What are you doing, Mr Larch?'

'Getting a nag for you and the kid,' he replied.

'Emily and I are not going anywhere.'

'Yeah?' Larch laughed. 'We'll see about that.' He thumbed back the hammer of the sixgun. 'Do as I say, Clooney.'

'Do it yourself, Larch,' he growled.

'I'll cut you down if you don't,' Larch snarled.

'You'll cut me down anyway.'

Larch had no intention of shooting Clooney. His plan to escape Apache revenge had sprung to mind with the ease of a brain well-rehearsed in skulduggery. His hope was that leaving Carver and Clooney behind to face the Indians would give him the time to make tracks for Eagle's Perch, an outlaw roost a couple of miles west of where he was. There he would find sanctuary. The outlaws of the roost often traded with the Indians and ran guns to them. Then, when the time was right and it was safe to travel, he would make his way to San Gabriel to check out the story about hidden gold. It was probably as Becca Carver had said, hokey, but he had nothing to lose by checking it out. As tradeable goods, he'd still have gold of sorts in Becca and Emily Carver. He planned to cross to Mexico, where some filthy-rich grandee would pay him handsomely for the diamond ring. He would then mosey along to Peru or Honduras where, with the cash from the sale of the ring, he would set up a brothel with Becca and Emily Carver as his first whores. Rich old men would pay plenty for a young girl. His life would be one of ease and luxury.

'Do as I tell you,' Larch told Clooney, 'and you can have one of those nags yourself.'

'What about Ned?' Becca asked.

'What about him?' Larch spat.

'What have I done,' Becca wailed.

Larch chuckled. 'Played the wrong hand, I'd say.'

'You're even worse than Clooney.'

'That,' Larch agreed, 'is perfectly true, Becca, my darling.' He turned to Frank Clooney. 'What do you say, Clooney. A horse for your help?'

The bounty hunter shrugged. 'It's a deal.'

Clooney jumped down from the wagon and began to unhitch the team. He figured that had Larch wanted him dead, he'd be dead long ago. He also reckoned, and correctly so, that Larch's plan was to leave him and Carver to face the wrath of the oncoming Apaches, while he made his getaway. Larch was counting on the Indians killing Carver and him slowly. That would give Larch time.

Clooney reckoned that Larch's plan was to

make tracks for the outlaw roost at Eagle's Perch.

The horses unhitched, Larch ordered Becca and Emily on board one. Then the evil that had rotted his soul oozed out of Spitter Larch, and he shot the second horse. He laughed.

'So I lied. It shouldn't take the Apaches long to home in on that gunshot, Clooney. Ride,' he ordered Becca.

'Hold it right there, Larch.'

Surprised, Larch swung about in the saddle. Ned Carver had come from the rear of the wagon, and was holding a cocked rifle on him. Obviously his wits were still scattered, which made him a very dangerous and unpredictable man. Instinctively, he recognized danger, but the way his rifle was switching direction between Larch and Clooney, his confused mind had not yet decided from whom the threat emanated.

Quick as a fox going to ground, Spitter Larch spoke.

'Are you going to let that no-good grab your wife and daughter, Ned?'

The clever use of Carver's first name immediately gave the impression of a friend looking out for a friend.

Ned Carver's rifle swung and settled on Frank Clooney.

'No, sir,' he declared, the glow of madness in his eyes. 'I am not.'

'Frank is not your enemy, Ned,' Becca said. 'It's Larch is doing the grabbing.'

'That's so,' Emily added.

'Frank?' Carver questioned, his confusion growing.

Becca explained, 'Sam Rafter is not his real name, Ned. His real name is Frank Clooney.'

Carver screwed up his eyes to study Clooney with new interest.

'The bounty hunter?'

'Yeah,' Larch said. 'And you know what kind of scum bounty hunters are, Ned.'

'Sure do, Larch. Had a brother gunned down by a bounty hunter, 'cause he held up a little old stage coach.'

'Never knew a bounty man who didn't need killing, Ned,' Larch said.

'Me neither,' Carver rasped.

'Maybe it's time to even the score for your brother,' Larch prompted.

Murder in mind, Ned Carver grunted.

'I guess it is at that.'

CHAPTER FIFTEEN

'Don't do this, Ned,' Becca pleaded with her husband. 'It'll be murder, plain and simple.'

'Don't waste your breath, Becca,' Frank Clooney said. 'Murder is nothing new to Carver.'

'It sure isn't, Ma,' Emily Carver said bitterly. 'He murdered Pa, remember?'

'I'm not likely to forget, Emily. But there's been enough killing.' She again addressed Carver, 'I tell you, Ned. Larch is our real enemy.'

'If that's so, why did you and Clooney plot to kill me?'

'The plotting was all mine, Ned,' said Becca.

'Hah! You expect me to believe that, woman?'

'It's the truth, Ned. And like I said, Larch is your enemy. He plans to kidnap me and Emily.'

Ned Carver wiped the persiration cascading off his forehead from his eyes. Larch grabbed his chance. The sixgun he had cleverly dropped to his side when Carver put in an appearance exploded. Carver was caught square in the chest. He shot backwards and crashed against the wagon. He slid down the wagon, his eyes fixed on the gaping hole in his chest.

'You ride with me, kid,' Larch told Emily.

'No,' Becca protested.

'She rides with me or I kill her now,' was Spitter Larch's ultimatum.

'Go to hell!' said Becca, defiant.

'I surely will,' Larch snarled. 'But not just yet.'

'Do as he says,' urged Clooney. Becca Carver's troubled eyes clashed with his. 'You don't have a choice, Becca.'

'Sensible advice,' Larch said.

'Even if you could stay here, there's those rene-gades to think about.'

Becca smiled sadly. 'I suppose I deserve no better than the devil's disciple, when I supped with Satan.'

'Move the nag,' Larch ordered Becca.

'Be sure to give Bold Eagle my regards now,' Larch taunted, as they rode away. He laughed. 'Before he rips your tongue out to stop you screaming.'

'I'll come looking, Larch,' Clooney promised.

'I don't think so, Clooney. I'd sure enjoy killing you, but I reckon that I'll enjoy more the thought of you in Apache hands.'

Larch held the .45 on Emily.

Gripped by a deep foreboding, Clooney watched the dust cloud come nearer. He had a crazy plan which might work. He could daub himself with Ned Carver's blood and try and fake death. However, if the ruse worked, which it probably would not, the result would be to put Becca and Emily in even greater peril than they already were, because the Apaches would have nothing to interrupt their pursuit.

The dust cloud, driven by a rising breeze, was suddenly swirling towards him. Clooney fetched the rifle he had hidden under the wagon seat. He had been tempted to fetch it as Larch rode away, but the outlaw was holding a gun on Emily. He might have got lucky; but Larch's finger might also have pulled the trigger in a reflex action.

Frank Clooney shot the first Indian who came into view.

Becca Carver heard the rifle shot and stiffened.

'Shame, that's what it is.' Spitter Larch chuckled. 'That mane of fair hair tucked inside an Apache belt, and you never getting the chance to run your pretty fingers through it, like you planned.'

'You must help him,' Becca pleaded.

Spitter Larch scoffed. 'Now why would I want to do that? I'd have to kill him then. Clooney is a dead man, Becca. Forget him.'

*

A second and third Indian were whipped from their ponies by Frank Clooney's deadly fire, in a defiant but token resistance. He did not know how many rounds the Winchester had left, but even if it had its full complement, his battle was already over.

He fired another two rounds, of which one found a target, before the hollow clunk of an empty chamber rang a death knell in his ears. He stepped from the cover of the wagon, inviting a quick demise, his heart full of the regret of not having a future with Becca, something he had begun to plan for and look forward to.

But the headlong charge for revenge did not materialize. The bitter-faced Apache shouting orders could be none other than Bold Eagle. His approach was measured. He dismounted and came face to face with Frank Clooney, to deliver a chilling promise.

'You will die slowly, white man.'

The bucks were already looting the wagon, where they found Becca and Emily's clothing. Their excitement reached new heights. One of the bucks drew Bold Eagle's attention to the fresh tracks made by Larch and Becca's horses. Clooney did not understand Bold Eagle's excited chatter, but he had no difficulty in getting its drift. The raiding party divided, half to haul him away, and the second bunch to pursue Larch, Becca and Emily.

A buck put a rope round Clooney's neck and hauled him half-running and half-dragged behind his pony. His guess was that they were headed for the canyon through which at one stage they had planned to flee. His guess was proved right, and there was only one consolation on seeing the renegade Apaches lurking in its rocky rises. To have tried to escape through the canyon would have delivered Becca and Emily to the Indians.

Frank Clooney did not understand Apache lingo, but when he saw kindling being gathered to start a fire, it was a case of a picture truly being worth a thousand words.

CHAPTER SIXTEEN

'Will you shut up, woman!' Spitter Larch snarled at Becca Carver. 'I told you a million times, I ain't going back to help Clooney. I don't feel like handing my hair on a plate to no damn Indian. Now you just stop your caterwauling, you hear? If you don't, I'll cut a fast trail and leave you and the girl for the Apaches to enjoy.'

Becca Carver trembled.

'Even you wouldn't do that,' she said, with a shake in her voice, knowing quite well that saving his own neck would take priority over everything else in Spitter Larch's book. His sly, cruel sneer confirmed her thinking.

Larch drew rein and climbed up a rocky slope to check out the immediate country. The flat desert had given way to a terrain of more variety, and more danger. He had made reasonably good progress, but there was still quite a way to go to the outlaw roost and safety. He reckoned that by now the knives of the Apache torturers should be scraping Frank Clooney's bones bare.

In his anxiety to put distance between him and the Indians, he had not covered his tracks. Might that have been foolish? He would have not travelled as far had he taken the time to do so. But he might have regained that time down the line if the Indians had to search for clues to find the direction he had taken. Of course, the Apaches, being born trackers, would pick up his trail no matter how well he disguised it, and he tried to take consolation from that fact now that his doubts about his strategy haunted him on seeing the plume of curling dust to his rear. The plume was not as thick as it had previously been, confirming his worst fears. A smaller and faster band of Indians had been assigned the task of running to ground whoever had taken flight. He was betting that they had also found Becca and Emily Carver's clothing, and knew that there were white women to be had as a prize. Such an incentive would make their zeal to hunt the fugitives all the greater. Scalps and white woman pleasures would drive them relentlessly.

Frank Clooney's fear stifled his breath. He could smell his fear oozing through his pores. He would not be human if he were not afraid. He had seen in the carcasses (for that was all the remains could be called) of men and women the Apaches had tortured, their terrible deaths and suffering etched in the rigors of their faces, jaws locked in stilled screams, eye-sockets empty, and yet it was not difficult to imagine those eyes filled with fear and pleading; a pleading that had gone unheeded.

Again, though he could not understand his lingo, Bold Eagle's gestures made his orders perfectly clear. The renegade's commands chilled the bounty hunter's blood to below zero. He was facing his greatest fear of all.

His eyes were about to be plucked out to render him utterly helpless.

Spitter Larch came scrambling down the rocky slope.

'Apaches,' he announced. He vaulted into the saddle. 'Keep up or lose your hair.' He set off at a quick pace.

Becca did her best to keep up, but being a town woman used to the leisurely life of a marshal's wife, she had never had a need to learn to ride a horse with the kind of expertise that keeping up with Larch needed. She lost ground and fell further and further behind, until Larch's panic subsided and he realized that his only chance of getting out of a bind if the Indians caught him up, was to hold a bargaining chip – like two white females. Besides, his nag's legs would not keep up the pace he had set. He fell back and allowed Becca to catch him up.

'I guess leaving you ladies to the mercy of the Apache would be a mighty ungentlemanly thing to do,' he said.

Becca held her tongue. She knew very well that Spitter Larch had not suddenly got a conscience. So there was only one reason that she could think of for him slowing his pace, and that was her and Emily's tradeability with the Indians. To say anything would only scare Emily more than she already was. And, also, it would be unwise to upset Larch, because their only hope of escaping from the Indians was to reach the outlaw roost he was headed for.

Becca Carver's thoughts turned again to Frank Clooney's plight; a plight she had played a big part in. Had she not ranted as she had when she discovered his deception and line of work, they would have made a lot of headway, and might very well have outpaced the Apaches. Now Clooney was probably dead, and before much longer it was likely that she would wish that she and Emily were too.

Frank Clooney kicked out at the Apache whom Bold Eagle had ordered to pluck out his eyes. His boot caught the eager buck in the groin. He howled, dancing around, his anger building to a white-hot rage. A couple of bucks came to his aid, but Bold Eagle held them back. He had been assigned to Clooney's disfigurement, and the buck would have to see his task through, even if it meant that Clooney would kill him. To Bold Eagle's way of thinking, if the buck was defeated by the white man, that made the white man the better of the two. It would not benefit him any, because Bold Eagle would simply order another Apache to fulfil the task which the first man had failed to complete. Or, if he thought his judgement might be questioned were the second buck to fail, he might take on the task himself.

Overcoming his distress the buck circled Clooney, his knife slashing the air inches from the bounty hunter's face as it swept back and forth, forcing him to dance back. The heel of Clooney's boot slid off the edge of a rock and he stumbled backwards. With his victim off balance, the buck saw his chance to get the trophy he so wanted to hand Bold Eagle, knowing that his standing in the renegade leader's eyes was now at its lowest, and his fellow Apaches would share Bold Eagle's opinion of him. Death would be preferable to being shunned.

Frank Clooney fought desperately to regain his balance, but it seemed impossible to do so. The patch of ground he was on had many rocks on which to stumble, and loose shale that rolled under his boots, taking his legs from under him. He fell. The buck was diving through the air, the hunting-knife ready to plunge into him.

A sudden gunshot blew the top of the Indian's head off. He crashed to the ground alongside Clooney.

Bold Eagle was holding a smoking rifle, but Clooney's optimism was not soaring. The buck's knife would have plunged into him, and it would have been over. Bold Eagle would no doubt prefer the slow death for the white man that he had planned.

Bold Eagle handed the rifle to the buck nearest to him, and slid a knife from his belt. Obviously, he was not going to entrust the task of plucking Clooney's eyes out to anyone else.

'Come on, you damn lazy nag!' Spitter Larch swore at the failing mare. He dug his spurs deep into the horse's flanks, but the beast was spent. Her eyes rolled wildly in her head and her legs wobbled and then buckled, pitching Larch from the saddle. For a couple of seconds the horse thrashed about, whinneying, before she went still.

The outlaw, swearing profusely, picked himself up, grimacing at the pains shooting through him after the heavy fall. The way he looked at Becca made her as cold as if an arctic wind had curled round her.

'One horse won't take three people,' he said. He grabbed Emily and pulled her from Becca's horse. He flung her roughly to the ground. 'The girl stays put,' he declared.

CHAPTER SEVENTEEN

Bold Eagle was a much wilier and more formidable opponent than the young buck had been. He could simply have had Clooney overwhelmed, but that would have given the bounty hunter a greater standing as a man, and lessen his. There were murmurings among the other Apaches when his choice of buck had proved unwise, and there was a need to redeem himself if he was to remain unchallenged as the leader of the renegades. He could not afford to have feet of clay, because the Apache were as ruthless with their own, who failed, as they were with any white man who transgressed.

Bold Eagle need not have worried. A bullet from high up on the rim of the canyon shattered his spine.

*

'No!' Becca Carver screamed, kicking out and scratching at Larch.

'Shush, woman,' he raged, and struck her. The force of the blow sent her tumbling. 'Like I said, the girl stays put!'

By now, traumatized, Emily Carver cowered on the ground. Larch hauled a stunned Becca to her feet and shoved her towards the horse.

'Please,' Becca pleaded. 'Leave me, take Emily.'

'And what am I supposed to do with a kid?' Larch scoffed.

'I won't go with you,' Becca declared defiantly. 'I won't leave Emily.'

Spitter Larch threatened, 'Get in the saddle now, or I'll kill the kid.'

Becca Carver was suddenly more weary than she had ever been in her entire life. It was as if in a blink the years had piled on to sweep her in seconds to old age.

'That would be better than leaving her to the Apaches,' she said.

'All the same to me,' Larch snorted.

In the seconds of confusion that followed on Bold Eagle's demise, several more Indians were dropped under a vicious hail of rifle fire. Clooney's eyes searched the top of the canyon for sign of his rescuers, but could only see the constant puff of smoke as the rifles continued to fire. He grabbed the rifle and ammunition belt of a fallen buck and sprinted for the rocks, firing from the hip as he raced for cover, from where he joined the siege.

It was a brief slaughter. The shooters on top of the canyon showed no mercy, and made every bullet count.

The gunfire spread out across the terrain to reach Spitter Larch's ears. It confused him. As far as he knew there were no soldiers in the immediate territory, because it was a condition of the truce that they withdraw behind agreed boundaries. So who was doing the shooting?

The Apaches in pursuit of Larch also paused to listen to the furious gunfire. They, too, knew that the gunfire could not be coming from the bluecoats. And theirs was the same question as Larch's. They swung around and headed back to the canyon.

'Hello, the canyon top,' Frank Clooney hailed. 'You surely have my thanks.' Three men made an appearance, and began to make their way down through the rocks. Clooney became uneasy in himself; an unease that grew with each passing second.

'Howdy,' the tallest of the three hailed. The man had a familiar cut to him. 'Saul Sweeney's the name.'

Clooney knew that he had simply traded one problem for another, and an equally deadly one at that. Once they came face to face, the Sweeneys would recognize him, and old scores would be settled. And on a three to one basis, there could be only one outcome.

Frank Clooney grabbed a loose pony. Riding bareback, he'd not be able to match the Sweeneys pace, should they give chase. But they'd take time to regain their saddles, and that would give him a good headstart.

Taken aback by Clooney's helter-skelter departure, Saul Sweeney roared:

'Damn your hide. You ungrateful bastard!'

Three rifles started blasting.

'Ma,' Emily Carver wailed, as Spitter Larch slid his sixgun from its holster.

To Emily Carver's amazement and sadness, her ma seemed to be indifferent to her plight.

'Ma!' she pleaded again.

'Don't whine so, kid,' Larch said. 'Your ma and me's got places to go, and we don't want no kid along.'

Becca Carver maintained her pose of indifference until Spitter Larch's gaze drifted away from her for a second. Then she grabbed a rock and slung it at him. Instinctively alerted to trouble, the outlaw ducked. The rock bounced off his

146

right shoulder. Painful, but the missile did no damage that he could not deal with. His eyes mere slits, glowing coal-hot with anger, Larch faced Becca and levelled the .45 on her.

Becca Carver took Emily into her protection, and stood staunchly defiant.

'Do your damnest, Larch,' she said. 'And damn your rotten soul to hell.'

Cutting a weaving gallop out of the canyon, Frank Clooney felt the breeze of the Sweeneys' bullets. Chased by lead, and having witnessed the Sweeneys' shooting skills at first hand, he could only pray that any luck that was going would be his. As he ate up ground, the threat from the outlaws' rifles became less. He was a mighty relieved man when he shook off the dust of the canyon, still in one piece. A time or two his head-long dash had almost unseated him. Riding bare-back needed lots of expertise; an expertise that was peculiarly Indian.

As his frenetic gallop to freedom achieved its purpose, Clooney slowed his pace to calm the excited pony. The pony knew that there was a strange load on its back, and was anxious to shed it.

'Easy,' Clooney coaxed. 'I mean you no harm.'

He rubbed the pony's mane, gently easing its apprehension. Soon, man and beast were friends.

Clooney could see no sign of pursuit, but not for a second did he believe that the Sweeneys would not give chase. They were riled, and riled good. And there were few, with the exception of Spitter Larch, more resolutely spiteful in settling a score than the Sweeney brothers. Normally they were vindictive, murderous bastards, and that was when they were in good humour. Now with their hackles up, they would be doubly vindictive and ten times more murderous.

Larch, knowing that to leave Becca and Emily Carver to the mercy of the Apaches would be sweet revenge for Becca's treachery, had to consider the possibility that they might somehow escape that fate. Therefore, to be certain, he would kill them now.

Becca Carver held Emily close to her and, closing her eyes, muttered a final beseeching prayer. Another burst of gunfire filled the air. Larch's eyes went every which way, trying desperately to pin down the source of the gunfire and gauge its distance.

The gunfire was a mystery. Who could be shooting at whom?

For the briefest of moments his hopes rose high. Maybe the US Cavalry had put in an appearance and had engaged the renegades. After all, with renegades on the rampage, sooner or later they would be forced to act – preferably sooner. But Larch's hope was short-lived, and he set that possibility aside. Hunting down the renegades would put the hard-won treaty in danger of collapse. The probability was that the army would let Indian bring Indian to book. But to Larch's way of thinking, an Apache was a damn Apache, and not to be trusted. Like most white men, he believed that the only good Indian was a dead Indian. And he figured that most Indians thought the same way about white men.

Larch changed his mind again, and went back to his former idea of having a trading-chip. But with only one horse, he could only take along either Becca or Emily Carver. Not both.

Frank Clooney could, he reckoned, if he was of a mind to, outride the Sweeneys. But he had a mission to accomplish first, Becca and Emily Carver's rescue. He returned to the abandoned wagon, where he picked up sign of shod horses, and one distinctive horseshoe with a flaw in the shape of a half-moon. These he tracked. Thankfully, Spitter Larch's urge to put distance between him and the Indians had not allowed time for him to cover his tracks.

Clooney knew that at any second he could run smack into the Sweeneys, or the Apaches who had gone after Larch. But his desire to save Becca and

Emily Carver from the terrible fate which threatened them drove him on, recklessly disregarding
danger to himself.

'I'm not moving one inch,' was Becca Carver's
fierce rejection of Larch's order to mount up.
'You're going to have to kill me, as well as Emily.'

'I ain't got no time for no nonsense,' Larch
raged. Striking out at Becca he brought her to
her knees. He grabbed her by the hair and
dragged her to the waiting horse. 'Now get on
board,' he growled. He put the barrel of the .45
against her forehead. 'I'll count to three. Then
I'll kill you and leave the girl for the Apaches.'

He thumbed back the sixgun's hammer.

'One . . . two . . .'

Inevitably, Clooney's reckless flight ended in trouble. Tracking through a draw, he sensed a presence. Looking up, he saw a duo of renegade
bucks watching him. Another couple of seconds
and he would have looked certain death in the
face.

Maybe he still did.

'OK. I'll do as you say,' Becca Carver told Larch.

A desperate idea that might just work had
come to mind.

'Thought you might,' Larch sneered.

Becca mounted up.

Larch walked to where Emily cowered.

'Goodbye, kid,' he snarled.

CHAPTER EIGHTEEN

The first Apache charged. His lance grazed Clooney's left shoulder. Before he could recover, the screaming Indian leaped from his pony and swept Clooney from his mount, his tomahawk poised to open the bounty hunter's skull as soon as they crashed to the ground. The second renegade watched contentedly, seeing no problem for his comrade in dealing with the white man.

Clooney, conscious of the disadvantage of colliding with the stony ground first, tried to turn the Indian. But the iron-muscled Apache resisted, and the result was that neither man crashed to the ground with clear superiority. They rolled, trying to soak up the pain as quickly as they could, to ready themselves for the fight once their roll on the hard ground came to a halt. When it did, the Apache had the slightest of chances to split Clooney's skull open, but the bounty hunter's quick reaction changed the odds again. He drove his knee into the buck's belly. The Indian doubled up. Clooney slammed a rock into the Indian's face. As the Apache went reeling backwards, he followed through with a crunching boot to the ribs. A splinter of shattered rib poked through his side. The Indian howled and fell hard on his back. His head collided with a boulder. The grisly sound of his fracturing skull sent a cold shiver through Frank Clooney.

The second renegade, surprised by the swiftness of his change of role from leisurely spectator to active participant, gave Clooney the vital seconds to grab the sixgun the dead Apache had tucked inside his belt, no doubt a trophy taken from a dead white man. The second Indian had his rifle levelled when the sixgun exploded. As he was blasted off his pony his rifle shot went harmlessly skywards.

Clooney cursed. His luck had been fickle. He had survived, but blasting guns would be heard. Fickle luck was dangerous luck. The next time it could switch sides.

Becca Carver charged.

Spitter Larch, confident that he had her spirit broken, was taken by surprise as the horse bore down on him. He side-stepped, but Becca swung the horse and collided with him. The force of the contact swept the outlaw aside. He spun off and fell awkwardly. Becca leaped from the horse, and before Larch could regain his wits, she landed a heavy blow with a rock on his head. The outlaw groaned and slumped unconscious or dead. Becca did not care either way. Up to the last second she had not been sure that her plan would work, but gave thanks that it had.

She rode away with Emily.

Becca did not have an idea where she was or where she was headed. Her only concern was to put distance between them and Spitter Larch. He might be dead. But he might also come to, seething with revenge.

Of necessity, after his close brush with death, Frank Clooney's progress was slower and more measured; he had constantly to check out the country ahead for sign of Indians or other murderous critters like the Sweeneys. The problem was that as the terrain become more varied opposing forces might meet up by simple bad luck.

A stiff breeze had blown up, making Larch's tracks more indistinct. In open stretches where the breeze was stiffest, the tracks vanished altogether, and Clooney was forced to rely on experience and good fortune in setting his direction. Also there was the problem of other tracks crisscrossing Larch's. His only sure guide to Larch's tracks was the horseshoe with the half-moon flaw. However, Clooney was forced time and again to dismount to check on Larch's trail. It was all time lost. And with the breeze on the verge of being promoted to a wind, soon there would be no trail left to follow.

As day slipped into night, Becca Carver took shelter in a cave. Emily had not spoken, and seemed incapable of doing so. The horrors her young mind had had to deal with had overwhelmed her, and she had retreated into a place in her own mind which, by her outward appearance, was calm and peaceful. At least that was something to be grateful for.

Becca sat at the mouth of the cave watching the rising moon, and wondering what her and Emily's fate would be. She watched for any sign of trouble, particularly in the form of Spitter Larch. She had, she hoped, put several miles between her and the vicious killer. But she was also conscious of the fact that she might have been going round in circles, and Larch might be only a stone's throw away.

There would be a full moon. At least that would light up the landscape.

Frank Clooney, also, was grateful for the full moon. His progress would be at a snail's pace, of course, but it was better than making no progress at all. The night would bring danger. Added to the previous threats to his well-being, he would now also have to worry about four-legged predators searching for a meal.

Clooney became aware of a change in the pattern of the tracks. Now there was only one horse. The indentation of the flawed horseshoe was not as marked, which meant that the load the horse was carrying had lessened. What could that mean? That Becca and Emily were riding, and Spitter Larch was walking? Unlikely, he thought. Larch was not one of nature's gentlemen, who would give up the comfort of the saddle for the distress of walking. Could it be that Becca and Emily had escaped from Larch?

A small flicker of hope began to take root in Frank Clooney's heart.

He was still nurturing that hope when, suddenly, a bloodied face reared up from the rocks in front of him. Moonlight glinted on the barrel of a sixgun.

'Well now, if it ain't Mr Clooney,' Spitter Larch snarled.

CHAPTER NINETEEN

'Just step down from that nag,' Larch ordered Clooney. 'Real slow.'

'Where's Becca and Emily?' was Clooney's concern. 'If you've harmed them, so help me I'll—'

'Shut up!' the outlaw commanded. 'And do as I tell you right now. Unless you want to argue with this Colt?'

Angry with himself for letting Larch get the drop on him, Clooney's instinct was to buck him. But he had never yet come across a man who was faster than a bullet. He dismounted.

'You didn't answer my question, Larch?'

'I ain't the kind of *hombre* who's used to answering questions,' Larch rasped. 'But I'll give Becca and Emily your kind regards before I kill them.'

'Did Becca do that to you?' The bounty hunter chuckled, pointing to the raking wound on the left side of the outlaw's head. 'Whupped by a woman,' he sneered.

Angered by his taunting, Spitter Larch almost fell into the trap Clooney had set, but drew back from his quickfire lunge.

'You'd like me to get close, wouldn't you, Clooney,' he snorted. 'Well, I can plug you from a horse. Same thing in the end.'

'I guess that's the safest bet for a stinking coward like you, Larch.'

The trap failed to work again.

Larch grinned. 'Sticks and stones, Clooney.' He mounted the Apache pony. The beast danced uneasily. 'Settle down, you damn nag!' the outlaw growled. He looked at Clooney with sudden interest. 'Nogales!' he declared. 'You were the hardass who came to that cantina whore's rescue.'

'Slow-witted bastard,' Clooney scoffed.

'*Adios*, Clooney,' the outlaw snarled, levelling the sixgun on the bounty hunter. 'Can't say that it's been nice knowing you. Tell Satan I was asking for him.'

The pony, still on the restless side and sensing danger, reared. With Larch unsettled, Frank Clooney lost no time in pulling him from the pony. He grappled with the outlaw, still threatened by the .45 he held. Slowly, irrevocably, Clooney turned the Colt into Spitter Larch's gut and pulled the trigger. There was a short choking sound before blood gushed from the outlaw's mouth. His last seconds of life were spent looking at Clooney, puzzled and unbelieving.

As Clooney resumed his tracking, he saw eyes glowing in the dark. It did not trouble him any that Spitter Larch was about to become a meal.

It was close to first light when Becca Carver woke, cursing that she had dozed. Of all the fool things to do! she rebuked herself. She scanned the immediate terrain, but she could not see much in the grainy first light. Then she froze, on sensing that there was someone in the cave behind her.

'Easy, Becca,' Frank Clooney said softly. She swung around, her joy bringing a flood of tears to her eyes. Emily was cradled in his arms. 'Emily was having a bad dream,' he explained. 'But she's sleeping peacefully now.'

Their journey was a long, arduous and horror-filled trek. A couple of days later they found three scalped and mutilated men, unrecognizable. Beside one of the men Clooney found a silver timepiece. When he flicked it open, the engraving read: *To Pa from Ma Sweeney on their wedding day.*

Clooney and Becca talked a lot on the journey. Clooney about how he had become a bounty hunter; Becca about her hopes for the future.

Slowly, Emily came round to join in. No one was sure how they ended up in Hawk Ridge. It happened that way, and just when the town marshal had retired.

'You wouldn't be the first bounty hunter to put on a badge, Frank,' Becca said, when the town council offered him the marshal's job.

'And,' Clooney kissed Becca, 'for a whole lot less a reason than I have.' Frank Clooney drew Emily to his side, with Becca on his other side. 'Does this town have a preacher?' he asked.